Chapter 1. The Captain's Table Again

Peter Barten was having a good day.

He was wandering back through Lincoln High Street, after a nice cuppa in the Skegness Pottery cafe at the bottom of Steep Hill.

Good old Skeggy Pot, they'd always looked after him when he was 'on his uppers', back when he was signing on at the Dole Office just around the corner. They'd always been good for a free cup of tea, and would let him nurse it for as long as he wanted... as long as they weren't busy.

Then it was always an apologetic,

"Sorry Peter, but we do need the table back."

Mind you, he had probably been sat there all afternoon, absorbed in the details of the decoration on their bespoke cups and saucers, and they were always very polite about it.

Things were very different now though. Not only could he afford the tea, he could splash out on a whole pot to himself, and if he was feeling very extravagant, would even treat himself to the odd cheese scone!

He wasn't one to throw his money around too much though. He didn't want to give the impression that he was suddenly loaded, and besides, little Mo would have had something to say about that.

Oh, didn't I mention it, the young, carefree Peter Barten, famous for his daring exploits, and infamous for his 'birds', has settled down.

Happily married with four kids, and driving a Volvo instead of a sports car.

Michel was to blame of course - he originally introduced Peter to Mary Jo - now his 'little Mo', back when they first flew into Socotra.

... And those two years Peter spent at Socotra hospital gave them lot of time to get to know each other. Mind you, it was obvious to everyone almost straight away where things were headed.

The hospital Padre married them before they left to return to the UK, and Peter somehow managed to persuade Mo that she really wanted to come to live in Bomber County.

"Lincolnshire's not that bad."

"It's flat, and boring."

"Not all of it. There a couple of hills in Lincoln itself, and besides, flat is good for Vulcans..."

They found a 'doer upper' in one of the few villages above sea level - a rundown old farmhouse about a mile away from RAF Waddington, and they initially spent their spare time making it their own family homestead. Then they went on to create a family, increasing the global population by adding in another four souls.

More about them later... at the moment Peter's feet are winding their way off in the direction of the Old J B.

There was always time to follow up a cuppa with a pint; and besides, he had an important meeting to get to.

* * *

The Old J B had needed a complete refurbishment after the last time Peter and his 'friends' had visited.

Actually, more like a complete re-build.

The sign outside was the same, but the intervening years had seen more changes than just the refurb.

The name for one thing. Everyone else called it The Brewer. Only Peter still called it The Old J B.

... The bar staff were new - if you can call a couple in their 70s 'new'.

Walter and Doris took it over whilst the brewery had it fixed up - you can say they had to take on a 'doer upper' as well.

Mo would argue that they had the easier job!

Daffyd the barman was no longer working there - he never came back after 'that day'.

He was last heard of heading to London, to take up a job in Soho. Something about:

"I'd rather take my chances with the Kray twins than face Peter's hulking friends again."

Not that the 'Hulks' were any friends of Peter - and Daffyd was on pretty safe ground, as the Krays were long gone. He just liked to exaggerate for effect.

In fact, Peter had seen Daffyd since, in full regalia as 'Davina Joy', his Drag Queen alter-ego, in the Soho club 'Boogis Street'.

Daffyd's alter-ego that is, not Peter's.

Although to be fair, Peter had been known to do a darn good 'Madame Butterfly' at the Officers Mess Christmas festivities, so never say never!

When Peter walked through the door, he was, to say the least, a trifle dismayed to see Jacques le Boustarde at the bar, with his trusted guard dogs, Hulk One and Hulk Two at his flanks.

They probably had been given real names by their loving mothers, but if they had, they had been long lost in the mist of time.

Peter decided that politeness was the better part of valour, so instead of his usually witty jibe, he threw out a simple;

"Hello Chaps. Long time no see."

The Hulks grunted something unintelligible back.

Le Boustarde though...

"Ah Peter, glad to see you again. Can I buy you a pint of Best, for old time's sake?"

That knocked the wind out of him more effectively than Hulk One's plate sized fists had done the last time they had a drink together in the Brewer.

Walter poured a pint of Best nervously for Peter, and as he handed it to him, you could see the shakes increasing to the point he spilt some... over Hulk Two.

"There's... there's not going to be any trouble is there, Peter..." Walter stammered.

Doris ostentatiously picked up a cricket bat from behind the bar.

"No Walter, there's not going to be any trouble. These young fellas know better than that.

Don't you boys?"

Doris had learned her bar skills in London, and not in the salubrious West End. She might not have met the Krays, but she'd dealt with a few 'wide boys' in her time. She was having none of their nonsense today.

"If you think you're going to mess around like the last time you were in here, then think again.

Or you can... Get Outta My Pub...."

Doris turned around to Walter and winked.

"I've always wanted to say that."

Hulk Two laughed.

"You're all right, missus. We've got no beef with Mr Barten today. He's positively in our good books. You can put the cricket bat away now."

Walter breathed again.

Peter sat down with his pint, more confused than he had been for a long time.

"I have no clue what the hell is going on here. I thought I was meeting someone for a new flying job."

"You are." said a voice from the table next to the juke box.

"Le Boustarde and his companions aren't here to threaten you, Peter. They are simply providing security for our 'little chat'. In a manner of speaking you could say that they are our personal security detail.

You could even say that, if you agree to our proposal, as of today, they would be working for you."

That explained why Le Boustarde was being so friendly. He was always one to suck up to his bosses.

How the tables had turned.

* * *

The voice by the juke box stood up and came over to Peter. He recognised the style of his coat.

It might not be the same bloke, but it was definitely the same organisation, the same species of 'Crombie Man' as before.

"Come out to the back of the pub, Peter. What we have to discuss is above their pay grade, and there are a couple of people you need to speak to."

Peter particularly like the 'above their pay grade' comment. He looked at Le Boustarde, and you could almost see him shrivel up, as he was casually lumped in with the Hulks.

Revenge is indeed sweet he thought, and he hadn't even raised a finger.

Much less painful this way. He could get used to it.

There was a large private beer garden at the back of the pub. In the evening it would be rocking to the sounds of local bands, but right now it was deserted. Just Peter, Crombie man, and a couple of serious looking blokes sat at one of the benches.

They had a tray of drinks in front of them. What looked like a good few pints each.

Today was about to get interesting.

Peter wasn't sure yet if it was going to be 'good' interesting, or 'bad' interesting.

As he was about to find out, it was actually 'very, very bad' interesting.

Chapter 2. Opening Gambit

"Peter, do you play chess at all?" asked 'Crombie man'.

"No, I'm more your dominoes type, less complicated, and there's something about playing pieces made up of dots, separated into groups, that appeals to an old Morse coder." Peter replied.

His first real job in the RAF was as an Air Electronics Officer, in the back end of a Vulcan; before he retrained as a pilot and went to sit up front in the 'good seats'.

He was really good at Morse - had a good fist and ears for it.

That made him think of the two hulks sat back in the bar, and he reflected that the pairing of the words 'fist' and 'ears' would have a rather different connotation in their sordid world - you'd have to add 'cauliflower' to the latter!

"You should take up chess, Peter. It gives a good sense of overall strategy, and oversight into an operation with complex moving pieces..."

"I'm not sure I like the way this conversation is going," said Peter, "those pints don't look particularly interesting now. I think I might take a pass on them if you don't mind."

With that, he turned to go back into the Brewer, to make his way out, but the door was now firmly blocked by his two hulking 'friends', only now they seemed to have lost their previous bonhomie... they definitely looked more like the two brutes he first met in here all those years ago!

"Mr Barten, what do you know about UNOOSA?"

This was from one of the two 'serious looking' blokes.

"You what?" Peter was getting seriously pee'd off now. First chess, now this. Was this meeting just going to be a series of ever more stupid questions...?

"Sorry mate, I don't know any Una Sue. I know about Una Stubbs, if that helps - she was in Worzel Gummidge if I remember correctly...

Anyway, since we haven't even been introduced yet, please let me go first. My name's Peter, Peter Barten, and I appear to be the local village idiot. Not unlike said Worzel it seems."

"Oh, please accept my apologies, Peter. We seem to have got off on the wrong foot. My name is Guy de Maupassant, and I work for a different branch of the organisation you bravely undertook some missions for, so I certainly don't believe you to be a village idiot.

I believe you to be one of the most intelligent and professional operatives we have ever sent into the field.

That's why I insisted we came to see you at this most critical moment in the world's affairs.

I work for the United Nations Office for Outer Space Affairs. Actually, you could say I am the Head of UNOOSA."

This guy was a good judge of people - he had clocked straight away how to get on the right side of Peter. First the tray of beer, and now a couple of strategically placed, overly extravagant compliments. It certainly worked a lot quicker than battering him unconscious...

Peter's interest was definitely piqued by the words 'Outer Space Affairs', but before he could speak, 'Crombie man' piped up. He had been warned about Peter's rather childish sense of humour...

"That's got nothing to do with dating beautiful green-skinned alien women, Peter."

"I wasn't even thinking it." he mumbled into his pint glass... but everyone around the table knew 100% that he was!

Guy went on:

"The United Nations Office for Outer Space Affairs is a section of the UN that 'promotes and facilitates peaceful international cooperation in space'.

We work to establish, or strengthen the legal and regulatory frameworks for space activities."

Peter's eyes must have started to glaze over... He suddenly became very intrigued by Guy's impressive handlebar moustache, and the little mini beard on his bottom lip. "He looks a little bit like Mark Twain", he thought...

Guy laughed, and took a great big swig of best beer.

"I can only agree with the expression on your face, Peter. So far this is pretty boring stuff, but that last bit is the real reason I had to be at this meeting with you today. I promise that it does get more exciting eventually, but you may want to down some more beer before the next bit."

That was a suggestion that didn't need to be repeated.

Peter downed his first pint, picked up a second, and suddenly feeling a lot more mellow than before, settled in for whatever came next. He remembered now how much he'd always hated mission briefings. There was always too much information.

Just tell him where to go, and what he was supposed to do.

That was when it would get exciting.

But before that, more 'crucial' information was headed in his direction:

"I won't insult you by asking if you've ever heard of the 1963 Partial Test Ban Treaty, Peter. That's because, apart from my section of the UN, there are maybe ten other people in the world who would know of it, and fewer still who know about the Article 4 compromise, that allows for departure from the treaty."

The beer was obviously starting to have an effect on Peter, making him more garrulous, or maybe just more stupid, because the next rather unfortunate words out of his mouth were;

"Strange that you mention the 1963 treaty whatsit - I recently got invited to go on Mastermind you know, when they heard how jolly clever I am, and that's just what I've chosen as my specialist subject."

Guy raised an eyebrow, smiled to himself, and added,

"I'm extremely pleased to hear that, Peter. I had no doubt about it, but I'm glad that you've just confirmed to us that you are absolutely the right man for this job.

As of today, you are about to become the leading global expert in the application of Article 4."

Peter's 'spidey senses' started tingling - he was pretty sure this was a business he would be better staying out of.

"Ah now, just hold your darned horses, I haven't said 'yes' to any job offer yet. I think we might all just be getting a wee bit ahead of ourselves here."

At that point, the second 'serious looking' bloke, who hadn't said a word up to that point, kindly chipped in with a useful question.

This was obviously to help Peter gain a fuller understanding of the 'job offer'.

"Tell me, Peter, what do you know about your liability to recall as an RAF officer?

Oh, and so we don't get off on a wrong foot, please let me introduce myself.

My name is Humphrey Godley. Air Vice-Marshal Humphrey Godley, and I'm very pleased to inform you that His Majesty is cordially inviting you back into his armed forces.

Under my direct command.

Welcome back to the fold, dear chap."

Peter quietly downed the last pint on the tray in front of him, and carefully scrutinised the bottom of his empty glass.

"What on earth are you looking for in there, Peter?" asked Guy.

"I'm looking for the King's shilling mate, because it seems I just got press-ganged back into the RAF."

It was Humphrey's turn to laugh now.

"Well, not exactly that. I think we're going to need some more beer. Actually a lot more beer."

* * *

"There's one thing I don't understand, Humphrey." said Peter.

"Just one?" laughed Humphrey.

"Oh, ha blooming ha, very funny I don't think." threw back Peter.

It's funny how after a few pints, the difference in rank between a lowly Flight Lieutenant, and a lofty Air Vice-Marshal didn't seem to matter. Just a couple of flyboys enjoying a bit of 'banter'.

"What's on your mind, Peter? And please just call me Humph.

Every time you call me Humphrey, I think I'm back to being 14, and my mum has caught me under-age drinking in the beer garden, around the back of the Blacksmith's Arms. She always called me by my full name when I was in trouble."

Peter was beginning to quite like the AVM.

"Well it's this whole 'liability to recall' thing. Now don't get me wrong, I was never going to refuse the job… well, probably wasn't going to refuse the job…"

"Peter, mate, you were halfway out the door already…"

"Ok, so maybe I was just taking my time about it, but the thing is… My understanding is that it's only RAF officers who completed their service, that are designated as Retired List Officers. I thought you had to be on that list, and getting your pension, to be liable for recall?"

"Listen to this Guy; we've got a regular barrack-room lawyer here. You know, the same chap whose eyes were glazing over when you started on about regulations and the like."

There wasn't a peep from Guy. He'd stopped drinking four trays of beer ago. He wasn't exactly asleep. More 'passed out'.

Before Peter could continue expressing his expertise on the King's Regulations, Humph got in first.

"I know what you're thinking Peter. I've seen your record. Unceremoniously kicked out, on the way to serve at 'Her Majesty's pleasure' in HMP Lincoln.

You can't see how a dishonourable discharge would put you anywhere near that list?"

"Yeah, that's about it. All those years I was 'persona non grata', literally everyone's kicking boy, and now I'm suddenly back in the good books."

"Well, to be honest, it wasn't easy. I ran it past the PM first, but they were having none of it... 'The man's a criminal, and a reprobate... Find someone else...' That's a direct quote Peter. Number 10 really don't like you at all. Something about 'bringing down the best PM we ever had...'

So I had to go over their head. I arranged a Royal Audience. One of the perks of my job is a direct line to the Head of the Armed Forces, and His Majesty was very happy to hear me out. Apparently the Palace doesn't have the same problem with you as Number 10. Probably related to the fact that 'Uncle Freddy' insists that they raise a toast to you every time they have a family get together. If he had his way, you'd be Sir Peter by now!

Anyway, to cut a long story short, His majesty simply has to sign a document to expunge your dishonourable discharge, that gets you designated as a retired List officer, and the RAF will reinstate your pension back to the day you 'retired' from the service."

You could have picked Peter's jaw off the floor.

"And, he's going to do that for me?"

"Not going to, old son. He did it the same day. He also signed this document for me as well."

Air Vice-Marshal 'Humph' Godley reached down and pulled piece of paper out of a folder in his briefcase.

Well more than a piece of paper.

It held the Royal Cypher of King Charles III, and the signature *'Charles R.'* at the bottom.

"That's your commission, back into the service. You just have to accept it..."

Like he had a choice!

Peter looked at the 'paper'.

He hadn't realised how much he'd missed the RAF until this moment. Now looking down at the document in front of him, he realised...

"Hang on Humph; you must have picked up the wrong folder. This isn't for the RAF, and it's not for a Flight Lieutenant. This is for a Commander Barten in the Navy."

"Yes, about that Peter. That's you all right.

My full title is Air Vice-Marshal Humphrey Godley, UK Commander of Space Command.

If you don't know it already, Space Command is a joint command. Personnel from the Royal Navy, British Army and Royal Air Force all fall under my command, and for this mission you need to be able to pull rank with the Navy chaps in particular - you'll find out why tomorrow. So for goodness sake, just accept the commission, Peter.

FYI, a Commander is the equivalent of a Wing Commander in the RAF, so congratulations, you just got promoted."

Peter sipped his last drop of beer - he was done for tonight, and from the table full of empty pint glasses in front of them, he could already tell that tomorrow morning his head was going to feel 'interesting'.

All he could think, as he slipped into oblivion was...

"Commander Barten...

The name's Barten, Commander Peter Barten..... "

He didn't know it yet, but he was going to meet 007 quite soon.

Chapter 3. Black Status

Strangely enough, Peter can't remember how he got home from the Brewer, or how he got into his PJs and climbed into bed.

He does remember being woken up by Mo at 6 o clock in the morning, when she pulled the curtains wide open. It was a bright morning, the sun was already up and streaming through the window, straight into his only just half alive eyes.

"There's a pot of tea on the bedside table for you love, but I don't think you've got time for more than a cuppa. Your friends are downstairs waiting for you already.

They said something about starting your new mission... and they said it was time critical, so would I wake you up...

Is there something you'd like to tell me, Peter?"

That was a question Peter had to answer, right now, if he stood any chance of Mo renewing his licence when their next anniversary came around...

"There is something Mo, but to be honest I'm a little fuzzy about the details."

"Dodgy fish course at the Mess again was it, Peter? Or could it have anything to do with these messages you sent me, sometime in the early hours of this morning?"

She held up her mobile, and there was a sequence of ever more blurry images of Lincoln High Street and Cross O'Cliff Hill.

Oh, thought Peter, that explains how I got home then, the old Brewer's stagger.

"This was the message I was referring to, Peter."

: NEW JOB OFCER AGN. SPACE:

Ignoring the 'friends' waiting downstairs, Peter and Mo finished the whole pot of tea. He explained to her as much as he could, and then they had the usual conversation. The one they always had before Peter went on a mission. The conversation that forces couples have over and over again. The missions may be different, but the details aren't important.

This was about Peter and Mo, and nothing else.

* * *

They drove Peter a mile or so up the road, until they passed through the front gates of RAF Waddington, sailing past the guards without stopping. The car then headed towards the hangars that Peter knew so well.

His old squadron, 101, had been based here, and even though the Vulcans had left Waddo many years before, part of him fully expected to walk into those hangars and see a host of V Bombers in all their glory.

... But the car pulled up between the hangars, in front of a group of four shipping containers; they were stacked two up, two down, and were all painted matt black.

"Your Operations Centre, Commander Barten. They are waiting inside to brief you now."

Peter hated briefings at the best of times, but this morning, manfully coping with the after effects of all the beer he consumed last night, he could really have done without this.

... And he could really do without a very chipper looking Air Vice-Marshal, bounding down the stairs from the upper containers, with an enormous grin on his face.

"Good morning, Peter. I hope you slept well. We've got lots to get through, and as you've heard, time is of the essence, so we'll dispense with any formalities in here.

Mind you, anywhere else on the airbase, it will need to be 'Yes Sir, No Sir', and you giving me your best salute Commander Barten. After all, we do have high standards to uphold..."

Humph's wink did rather give the game away though.

"I brought you a mug of coffee. Strong and black. I thought you might need it.

Shall we get going? I'm sure you're keen to find out what this is all about."

The inside of the Ops Centre was as bleak as the outside. It looked like it had been cobbled together from any old chairs and tables that could be spared from the rest of the base.

At least the internal walls were white, not black. Most of the tables were covered in communications equipment, but there was one table that had been left clear.

Clear that is if you ignored the copious supply of coffee and chocolate biscuits.

Things were looking up for Peter.

"First things first, Peter, let me explain about the set up here, then Guy will go over the background to this mission.

You are currently sat in the beating heart of your operation..."

Peter looked around. This looked less like a beating heart, more like a telemarketing call centre.

"... The team here can get in contact with any military personnel, any civilian or any government agency; and they will be able to contact you immediately, wherever you are.

... And that does mean anyone Peter. You can literally contact anyone alive on earth today."

Now I've heard it all, thought Peter.

"You mean I could call the PM, or POTUS, and they'd take my call?"

"Yes Peter, they would."

Peter turned around to one of the Communications Specialists and asked;

"There's a lass I dated a few years back, we lost touch, and I keep meaning to see how she is. I don't suppose you can get me a recent number for her..."

"Hmm, if we can keep on task, please Peter," continued the AVM.

"I don't know if you noticed on your way in, but this quadrant of the airbase has been sectioned off, and is being guarded by an RAF Regiment field squadron, which has been placed under your direct command. They are now allocated to Black Wing. This quadrant of the airbase is now Black Station, and you, Peter, are Black Commander.

I'm going to hand over to Guy now, to fill in some background."

Before Guy could start though, the Comms Specialist came over to Peter, and handed him a printout.

: LISA WALKER. RESIDENT BERWICK UPON TWEED. TELEPHONE NUMBER......

Peter scrunched the printout into a ball and lobbed it into a waste bin before he finished reading it. He couldn't risk Mo's spidey-sense picking up on that!

Guy watched the ball of paper arc into the bin, gave a weary sigh, and started with the background before Peter went off on another tangent.

Last night he was convinced Peter was the perfect person for the job. This morning he was starting to have second thoughts, but it was too late now.

"Yesterday, I mentioned the Partial Test Ban Treaty, and Article 4 of it.

The treaty is formally known as the 1963 Treaty Banning Nuclear Weapon Tests in the Atmosphere, in Outer Space and Under Water. It prohibits all test detonations of nuclear weapons except those underground.

Article 4 of the treaty was drawn up later, when a compromise was struck to allow departure from the treaty. In simple terms, it grants parties the right to withdraw if extraordinary events have jeopardised the supreme interests of its country.

Yesterday, while we made contact with you, there was an extraordinary meeting of the United Nations General Assembly, and a motion was passed, formally invoking Article 4, to allow for a nuclear detonation beyond the atmosphere of the earth."

He didn't know whether it was the coffee, or what he'd just heard, but Peter's mind was suddenly as clear as a bell.

"So, we're going to detonate a nuclear device in Space, to counteract a threat. A threat which is 'jeopardising the supreme interests' of the United Kingdom?"

"That's a pretty good summary, Peter. It's close, but it's not quite the whole story.

At the United Nations meeting yesterday, every single country asked for the Article to be invoked.

Every country on earth is under threat.

We are currently at Global Threat Status: Black."

Chapter 4. The President's Chair

The auditorium at the United Nations building was a busy place.

Mrs Enkhe Ogilvie was sitting in the President's chair, as she was acting in that role for this session.

She would normally have been sitting as the Mongolian Representative, but the convention since the last permanent President, Mr Lee Akina Luanda, was for the Acting President to become the representative for the country of Shatt El Arab.

The President's chair was the same plain, common wooden chair that Mr Luanda had used; the only addition was a couple of cushions to make it a bit more comfortable.

They had been gifted to the President's office by the representatives of Iran and Iraq.

The first of the two beautiful silk cushions had been purchased many years ago from a stall in the Old Bazaar of Bandar Abbas; and the second one from the Souq Al-Mubarakiya, the Old Basra Market....

Enkhe opened the extraordinary session of the United Nations General Assembly, and called on the only invited guest to start their presentation.

Dr Julie Davies wasn't used to speaking to large groups of people.

In fact she hated it.

The day she'd presented her PhD thesis, she had thrown up before she went in to the room.

Not because she was worried about her work, she knew that was solid, and even the galactically mean Professor Price was going to struggle to find anything to pick on; it was simply the thought of speaking out loud to a room full of people.

The only time she enjoyed speaking out loud to anything was in the observatory, chatting away to her celestial friends.

Mind you, she had got a bit better at public speaking since taking up the NASA post, but even then it was normally just to her team.

... And there were only the three of them.

But this was somewhat of an emergency, and unfortunately for her, she was the only NASA physicist free to fly to the UN to make this presentation. Everyone else was either on holiday, off sick, or 'rather busy' that day...

Besides, she was the 'new girl' and she'd definitely been handed the short straw.

Not that you really needed an astrophysicist to tell the UN representatives what had happened - but the seriousness of the situation meant that the UN President wanted someone with a bit of clout, and apparently Julie was that person.

She just hoped she didn't let everyone down.

"Representatives, I will try to make this as brief as possible, as I know you all have an important decision to make…"

Well, that's off to a good start, Julie thought to herself, now it's just the science to explain…

"The ISS blew up, and it's going to crash onto a city somewhere, probably killing millions of your citizens…" she blurted out.

"I mean… I'm sorry… I'm nervous…"

… And she was about to throw up…

Enkhe got up from the President's chair and carried a waste bin up to the lectern.

"Take your time child, we already had that information, although it hadn't been explained quite so succinctly."

She gave Julie a wink,

"Please, if you are able. Explain to us just as succinctly, what is the damage; describe to us the risk, and advise us of anything that we in this auditorium can do to help."

Julie pulled herself together. She thought of the advice that her Great-Aunt used to give her, and mentally 'put her big girl's pants on'.

"Thank you, Madame President. Please accept my apology. Let me continue:

At 01:00 UTC this morning, there was an explosion on board the International Space Station. The structure is now split into two sections, with the ROS breaking away from the rest of the ISS.

Unfortunately the Russian Orbital Segment houses the Data Management System, which handles guidance, navigation and control for the entire station.

At least it did, until yesterday. The explosion knocked out all power on the ISS, and completely destroyed the DMS.

Both sections are now in uncontrolled spins, which has increased the rate of their orbital decay.

When we have enough information, we should be able to calculate the new orbital decay rate, to give a more accurate picture, but that is really just an academic exercise.

With no prospect of us regaining control of the ISS sections, we won't be able to do anything about it.

To be clear, the ISS is bigger than a six bedroom house, with a total mass of 450,000 Kg. It is now less than 250 miles above the surface of the earth, and it is falling out of the sky."

Dr Davies had definitely pulled herself together, and had the full attention of the auditorium now.

"Unlike the managed deorbit undertaken for the MIR Space Station, it will not be possible to plan for where the ISS sections come down.

We know that some of the structure will burn up in the atmosphere; but there will be very large sections that reach the surface. We can calculate the impact forces based on the mass of each ISS module.

Let me quantify the risk for you. The ISS completes one orbit approximately every 90 minutes, in a progressive pattern. This means that it passes over 90% of the Earth's population.

Over almost every major city; and we do not know yet where it will hit.

If it lands on a city, the death toll will be enormous."

She took a sip of water, and continued;

"But I do have some good news for you.

With regards to the crew, most of them were in the main section of the ISS, and were able to escape. They safely evacuated, and have already returned to the surface."

The President stood up, nodded to Julie and said,

"Our thanks Dr. Davies. I certainly understand the severity of the situation a bit more fully now.

I have a couple of questions, if you don't mind.

You said that most of the crew managed to evacuate. Are you saying that there were some fatalities in the explosion?"

Julie hadn't been looking forward to this bit at all...

"No, I'm sorry to have to inform you, especially the Ukrainian and Russian representatives, but two cosmonauts were trapped in the ROS.

We know that they were alive last night when the crew evacuated, as they were able to seal themselves into the Nauka module. They were watching from the observation window as their colleagues escaped.

NASA is currently exploring possible rescue options, with all other national space agencies, and with the private launch service providers.

Nobody has a launch vehicle ready to go, but they are working together to prepare a rocket in the shortest timeframe.

To be honest with you though, the only timeframe that really matters relates to the breathable atmosphere in the Nauka module.

Without knowing the full extent of any damage, we can only make a calculated guess, but we think the cosmonauts initially had enough air for approximately 112 hours.

The time here in New York is 08:15, which is 12:15 UTC. They have already used up more than 11 hours of air.

Realistically, the chance of reaching them in time is probably not much greater than zero."

The auditorium went completely silent.

Enkhe looked over at the Representatives for Ukraine and Russia,

"Our thoughts must be with our colleagues, at what is a terrible time for their countries.

Thank you Dr Davies, I understand how difficult this is for you.

One final question.

In your opinion, is there anything else we need to know?"

This was the bit that Julie had been really dreading…

"Each of the two sections of the ISS has a Micro Modular Reactor on board.

These are small nuclear fission reactors, each containing a uranium-235 radioactive core.

When those sections make landfall, they will in effect become very large, and very efficient radiological dispersal devices.

So, to add to what I said before…

Every country represented here is facing the threat of an enormous great Dirty Bomb exploding in the middle of one of its major cities…

…. And of course, there will be two of them."

The auditorium suddenly became very frenzied.

* * *

Enkhe grabbed Julie by the arm, and said;

"We need to talk."

She walked Julie out of the auditorium, and took her into an office next door.

Enkhe went up to one of the secretaries and demanded,

"Get hold of someone from the Office for Outer Space Affairs. I don't care who it is. Just get me someone on speaker phone now."

The secretary pressed a button on their phone, and only a few seconds later a voice came on the line.

"Madame President, my name is Guy De Maupassant, how may I help?"

Mrs Enkhe Ogilvie was not someone who just accepted things. She was a 'roll your sleeves up and sort it out' sort of a girl,

... And she was unwilling to accept that there was nothing on Earth that could be done, to save the two men stranded on the ISS.

She was straight to the point.

"Guy, I don't want to hear from you that there is nothing we can do...

Tell me very simply how we can bring down two people from Space. I believe that's your area of expertise, is it not?"

She didn't hear Guy's chuckle, because he sensibly covered his mouth, but she heard very clearly what he had to say next.

"Actually, Madame President, there is quite a great deal we can do. Without sounding impertinent, I'm glad you called me just now, as you saved us a couple of minutes.

I am about to board a helicopter, en route to pick up a colleague; and we are heading to a meeting about precisely that.

Can I call you back once I am in the air?"

With that Guy rang off, and Enkhe stared thoughtfully at Julie.

"I pulled you into this office, because I was going to suggest that you act as liaison with UNOOSA, in case there was anything the UN could do to help, but it looks like events are moving a lot more quickly that I expected. Will you please stay with me? I would like you in the room when our new friend Guy calls back."

Before Julie could answer, the phone rang. Enkhe didn't even wait for the secretary to pick up, she grabbed the phone and stated simply,

"Speak to me Guy, and call me Enkhe, we don't have time for titles."

"Ok, Enkhe, I'll try to keep this brief. My team woke me when the explosion on the ISS occurred, as they had been monitoring communications, and heard the evacuation order. Since then we have been in contact with the five space agencies; NASA, Roscosmos, JAXA, ESA and CSA, and we have a plan in place. I took the liberty of acting on behalf of the UN, as we have some assets that we don't widely advertise, but which could be quite useful in the present crisis.

I can go into details later, but you need to know that I have offered the services of some rather specialised equipment we maintain; that can reach the ISS in time to undertake a rescue mission.

I am now with the head of UK Space Command, and we are on our way to pick up a key member of personnel.

The United Kingdom has offered to provide any logistical support we require..."

Enkhe interrupted,

"Why the Brits, Guy. They don't have anything to do with the ISS, since they pulled out of ESA. Why not USA Space Force?"

Guy didn't hide his chuckle this time...

"Let's just say that the 'key member of personnel' has some issues that are best handled by his countrymen...

However, Space Force and a few others will be joining the party, so to speak.

Let me outline the plan, as you are going to need to pull a few strings.

You need to get up to speed on the 1963 Partial Test Ban Treaty, and its Article 4 compromise; and most importantly, the 1967 Outer Space Treaty.

But before that, I need to update you on the threat from the ISS.

There is a little detail that dear Julie was not made aware of before she was sent off to New York.

What she wasn't told... is that we also have the slight problem of another global pandemic to worry about..."

* * *

Guy spent the next five minutes explaining his plan to Enkhe, and she went straight back into the auditorium to call the Assembly to order.

None of the Representatives had left the room, since Enkhe had not formally ended the session when she walked out less than quarter of an hour before.

Every one of them watched as she went back to her seat, and took hold of the microphone in front of her.

"Colleagues, I have just received an update about the situation onboard the ISS, and it is a great deal more grave than we thought.

We are in a great deal of peril, so I address you now as a colleague.

We are all in this together, and we must work together to face this peril.

You should be receiving to your monitors a summary, in your own languages, about a threat that I became aware of a few minutes ago.

Please read it now, and speak out if there is any confusion about the issue. There can be no room for any misunderstanding today."

The information on their screens was short, and to the point. There was no misunderstanding.

"You should also see a plan that the United Nations has developed alongside the armed forces of most of the nations represented here today. This plan also only came to my attention within the last few minutes, but I have given it the full backing of the Presidency of the United Nations, and I urge you to give it your unanimous backing.

Representatives, we do not have time to delay. I will give you two minutes to digest the information, and then I will make the proposal that you can see detailed before you."

After exactly two minutes, Mrs Enkhe Ogilvie stood up from the President's chair and made a carefully worded proposal;

"I stand, not as the Acting President of the General Assembly of the United Nations, but as the Representative for Shatt El Arab.

I propose that we formally invoke Article 4 of the 1963 Treaty Banning Nuclear Weapon Tests in the Atmosphere, In Outer Space and Under Water.

I propose we invoke Article 4 of the Treaty, for the specific purpose of a single test detonation in low Earth orbit.

Who will act as seconder for this Proposal?"

Every hand in the auditorium was raised.

Chapter 5. The Hybrid

This just doesn't add up, thought Peter...

"Look, I know I'm not the sharpest tool in the box at the best of times, but I'm not totally daft either.

As far as I know, we've never been at Global Black before. That's like setting the hands of the Doomsday Clock at one second to, and the closest we've ever been before is 90 seconds to midnight.

So what is it that you're not telling me?"

Humph answered that question.

"Peter, we will tell you, but I think Guy needs to explain from the beginning. Things have been moving extremely fast, and you need to be properly briefed right away.

Your next few days are going to get very hectic, and very dangerous.

I suggest you grab a mug, and a plate of chocolate biscuits, and settle in for a few minutes."

Peter grabbed a plate, shoved a biscuit in his mouth, and washed it down with a swig of coffee.

"OK, I'm all ears. Tell me the worst."

Guy took it from there.

"Yesterday morning, at 01:00 UTC, there was an explosion on the International Space Station, which ruptured the structure, separating the Russian Orbital Segment from the rest of the station.

Both sections suffered severe damage, and consequently all power has been lost, and there is no attitude control.

The sections of the ISS are falling out of orbit, and we have no way of controlling where they hit.

There are two cosmonauts trapped in the ROS, and as of now..." Guy looked at his watch, "they have approximately 82.5 hours of air left.

There are two nuclear reactors up there, that will eventually come down to the surface.

So we are looking at a couple of Dirty Bombs, possibly headed to a couple of major cities...

... But the issue that's got everyone pretty hot and bothered, and the reason for all of this..." Guy gestured around the room.

"There are some rather nasty strains of germs being cultured in the Bio Lab, or as the ISS crew called it, the BIO HAZARD LAB."

He gave Peter a second to take that on board, then continued.

"One of the active experiments was using CRISPR gene editing to create a new genetically modified organism. You don't need to understand exactly what they were doing Peter, but I'm sure you'll have heard of GM crops etc. It's the same process.

They successfully managed to combine the genes of the Yersinia pestis organism with Streptococcus bovis to create a new hybrid organism. They chose that combination of organisms because AI modelling had predicted that they would produce a synergistic effect. That is, the combination of the two is greater than them separately.

If you think of radiotherapy and chemotherapy, they are individually very powerful, but in the right combination, they can increase their effects ten-fold."

Peter interrupted Guy, "If I am picking you up correctly, you're saying that someone up there has made a turbo-charged organism, and in all that medico-babble, I'm sure I heard 'Streptococcus'. So you are saying that there is a turbo charged bug up there. You're saying that someone has been messing around, and created a biological warfare agent...

Just how dangerous is this turbo-charged Streptococcus?"

Guy again, but now with a pallor that he didn't have before, and his voice cracking, as if he didn't want to say the next words aloud.

"The Strep part of the organism isn't the issue, Peter. They only chose that because it is highly infectious to humans, and can infect the oropharynx; the back of the throat.

They wanted an organism that they could spread through breathing - an airborne pathogen, and that's what they achieved.

The real issue is the other piece of the hybrid.

The other organism, Yersinia pestis, is not normally spread through the respiratory tract, but even so, it is pretty nasty.

Its normal route of spread is by flea-bites.

The last time there was a big outbreak of it, half the population of Europe were killed.

Peter, Yersinia pestis caused the bubonic plague epidemic,

It caused the Black Death...

... And this version, as you say, has been turbo-charged.

The new organism is an untreatable, unsurvivable strain of the Black Death; and the AI modelling predicts that it will wipe out the entire human population within two generations.

If it gets to the surface of the Earth, it will cause a Human Extinction Event."

* * *

Guy continued.

"There was supposed to be a failsafe in place. Once the ISS reached the end of its usable life, then the Bio-Lab module was to be launched out of orbit. Once it was in deep space, the plan was for it to self destruct, theoretically vaporising all the experiments.

Unfortunately that option is not available to us now, as we don't have any control over the ISS; and even if we could employ the self destruct, we can't be 100% sure that there would be complete vaporisation, and that none of the Black Death Hybrid would reach the surface."

* * *

After Guy had finished speaking, the table in the Operations Centre of Black Station was silent.

But not for long.

Peter stood up, poured another coffee, grabbed another biscuit, and said, in his best 'we've got work to do' voice.

"Guy, thanks for the briefing. That was one of the better ones, short and succinct. A bit depressing I have to say, but I guess that all of this..." He gestured around the room, "... hasn't been cobbled together just so that you could tell me a story to give me nightmares. I reckon you've hatched a cunning back up plan between you, and I suspect that muggins here..." Peter pointed at himself, "is going to be at the sharp end of Plan B...

... And I'm sure I heard the words 'hectic' and 'dangerous' just now."

Humph grinned at Peter, "Actually my old chum, my exact words were 'very hectic' and 'very dangerous', but you're right, we do have a plan. My turn to talk I think."

He stood up and beckoned Peter to follow him.

"Let's walk and talk."

He headed out of the Ops room. Peter followed him and they walked over to Hangar One.

"Peter, you already clocked that we're going to detonate a nuclear device in Space. Actually, technically it will be in low Earth orbit. That bit of the plan is relatively simple. You fly a device up there and point it at the ISS. It blows up, vaporises the ISS, the nuclear reactors and the Black Death Hybrid. As the meerkats say, 'Simples'."

Yeah, dead simple, thought Peter.

But he kept walking, and listening.

"One big problem we have, is that after the explosion yesterday, the two parts of the ISS are falling out of orbit rather more rapidly than we would like. That's why we have wasted no time putting all of this together.

Normally, atmospheric drag reduces the altitude of the ISS by about two kilometres per month. To keep it in orbit we have to perform orbital boosting, by routinely firing the main engines of the service module.

After the explosion, we have no way of performing an orbital boost procedure, and we now have the added problem that with the two sections spinning uncontrollably, the atmospheric drag has increased.

To put it bluntly, the current status of the ISS orbit is that no one has the slightest clue about how quickly the sections will fall to the surface…

However, the more timely problem Peter, is how you can save those two cosmonauts before their air runs out.

Then you just carry on with Plan B, and kindly vaporise the ISS for us."

Peter stopped in his tracks. "Did you just say I've got to nuke the ISS. I thought we would use a missile?"

"We will… that is to say, you will use a missile. You're just going to have to fly it into orbit first, and then if the plan works out, undertake a little space walk to save our cosmonaut friends.

Once they are safe and sound, you simply launch the nuclear missile from your aircraft; actually, at that altitude we should really call it a spacecraft, and you high-tail it home.

As I said 'Simples'.

You'll probably get a medal for this mission Peter."

"You've got to be kidding, Humph."

Not about the mission, Peter could believe that 'they' would quite happily ship him up into orbit, turf him out into the void of space, and detonate a nuclear device in close proximity to his rapidly aging body.

No, it was the medal bit he didn't believe for a minute.

More than likely someone sat in a comfortable office chair, in air conditioned luxury, would get a medal if the mission was a success, and a global catastrophe was averted; but you could bet your bottom dollar that it wouldn't be yours truly!

With that thought, Peter walked into the hangar.

His jaw nearly hit the floor again. He was literally dumb-struck at the sight of the aircraft in front of him.

He could hear the echo in his head of the moment when he and Ray had first set eyes on his last aircraft, his 'souped up' ex display Vulcan... Zero One:

'"Good Lord, look at that." Raymond responded first. It was unbelievable. I just gazed at it. I can still remember that vision to this day. It was bright silver from refuelling probe to fin top, and glistened in the arc lights.'

This was, if anything, more unbelievable.

Peter gazed at the machine in front of him.

It was lit up by directional spot lights, embedded in the hangar roof.

Except it would be wrong to say 'lit up'.

It looked like an enormous shadow, a looming presence in the hangar.

No, not like a shadow.

It seemed to actually suck light in from the spotlights, not allowing any to escape.

It was like a black hole, deforming space-time in front of his eyes.

"Peter, how do you like your new ride.

Say hello to Tango One."

Chapter 6. Tango In Black, With Shades of Grey

Peter looked at the aircraft in front of him, still unmistakably 'Vulcan-shaped', but somehow much more Dan-Dare than before.

The wings still had the curved leading edges that smoothed their way into the fuselage, which he had seen on Zero One, but the wing tips now had a sweeping curve downwards as well.

The engines looked very different; he didn't recognise them at all, but at least they were still set into the wing roots.

The black surface was completely smooth... even the refuelling probe was gone.

"Let's just hope it has big enough fuel tanks!" Peter said to himself.

Someone put a hand on his shoulder.

"You don't need to worry about that old friend. Come up into the cockpit with me and I'll tell you all about it."

Peter span around with a big grin.

"Bob Marshal. As I live and breathe. Well if you've had anything to do with this beauty, then I can breathe easy!"

As they climbed up into the cockpit, Bob carried on speaking.

"Peter, this is a Vulcan Mark 007. Do you remember me telling you that we had it in development?

The 007 designation is a nod to the team who developed the engine used for the HOTOL modification we put onto Zero One for you, but we've taken this Vulcan a step further.

These engines are the next generation on from the HOTOL engines. What you have now are synergetic air breathing rocket engines. These SABRE engines are capable of reaching Mach 5 flight in the atmosphere; but then they can close off to run as pure rocket engines...

Peter, they can take you to orbital velocity.

This isn't an aircraft. This is a space plane."

Peter sat down in the pilot's seat, and let out a slow whistle.

"So it is a 'Dan Dare' machine."

He looked around the inside of his new space plane.

The cockpit didn't look that different to Zero One. Still a single pilot's seat, and the same control joysticks. Multiple VDUs of course, but no switches on the fuselage walls for fuel pumps, cabin pressurisation systems, or the other functionary systems with which to operate the aircraft.

Bob saw him looking.

"It's all voice activated Peter. Actually it's all controlled automatically by the on board computers, but the pilot does have the option to override the system if required... if we trust you with the codes that is," he said with a wink.

"To be serious though, the system now has multiple redundancies built in, so it pretty much looks after itself, and will keep you safe. You just need to do the flying.

Except of course the auto-pilot is pretty foolproof as well..." He looked over at Humph, who had climbed up into the cockpit with them.

"Remind me again why exactly we needed to bring Peter on board?"

"I thought that was obvious Bob. We need someone to blame if it all goes horribly wrong."

Peter gave a nervous laugh to that. He really hoped they were joking...

Then he looked over at the back of the cabin and let out a proper guffaw.

There was a couch bed, and some bright spark had painted a white line around it, on the floor and wall of the cabin. They had also painted onto the couch itself:

: RAY SAFE ZONE:

"He would have appreciated that. The great lump spent most of his time lying on the couch whilst I did all the hard work..."

Bob laughed with him.

"I think you'll find that is the most critical piece of equipment on the aircraft." Then more quietly, "I was sorry to hear about Ray. You must miss him."

Peter said thoughtfully, "I think he would have enjoyed this whole bunch of shenanigans. He was always looking for a bit of adventure. We could be in the middle of an ocean, or in the desert, and he'd still be asking me if I wanted to go out on the town.

I was supposed to meet him that night for a few drinks, and then for whatever else he managed to drag me into.

He called and said he wasn't feeling too well, so was going off to his scratcher early. Asked me would I mind if we went out another night instead.

He never woke up. Cardiac arrest..."

Peter gave a nod to the heavens,

"Fly safe mate."

He looked back at Bob,

"Anyway, what's with the black paint job?"

* * *

"Oh, you noticed that did you, Peter?" joked Bob.

"I'm sure you can remember the briefings we gave you about the silver coating on Zero One, but let me remind you:

The silver covering had stealth properties so it couldn't be picked up by RADAR. Those transmissions were affected by the silver film, which had a high refractive index, and nothing was reflected back to their receivers.

All microwaves, x-rays and the vision spectrum frequencies were totally refracted by the silver atoms. As we said at the time, 'it would take a supersonic bat flying at ninety thousand feet to find the aeroplane'.

Well we've given that an upgrade.

The black 'paint' is a layer of graphene over the original stealth covering. We have added a two dimensional sheet of carbon atoms to enhance the refractive properties of the underlying silver atoms, and it produces an almost perfect absorption material.

That's why when you look at it, you get the feeling that it is virtually sucking the light in. It's as if you are staring into a light void."

Peter looked confused.

"OK, I get all that. But if the aircraft's jet black, then why the 'Tango' moniker? Tango makes me think of orange."

Now it was Humph's turn to laugh.

"It's T for Thunder Peter, we thought you'd appreciate it.

We had to come up with a call sign for the new squadron, and after discounting 'SS' for Space Squadron and 'SOS' for Space Orbital Squadron… although Bob was quite keen on SOS, given the state you brought Zero One back for his team to fix up last time… we started thinking about Vulcan, and his blacksmiths' hammer, but eventually ended up with a different hammer wielding God…

Thor, the God of Thunder."

Peter grinned.

"Thunder Squadron. Yes, I like it. But in my new all powerful role of Black Commander, I do have one slight change to make to it; and if you haven't yet assigned a squadron number, can I make a suggestion…

* * *

So Thunder Squadron became known informally as the Thunderbirds.

Peter also insisted that they were designated as 163 Squadron.

163 was latterly used for a Mosquito Night Striking Force Squadron, which was disbanded at the end of WW2, and neither Humph nor Bob could work out the relevance to the current work of Black Wing.

When they asked Peter, he tapped the side of his nose.

"That, my friends is definitely 'need to know'. Highly classified and above your pay grades I'm afraid. Strictly limited to the Barton Crew."

* * *

Bob spoke again.

"Peter, sorry to rush around so much, but time is pressing, and there's another old friend you need to meet right now, they're in Hangar Two."

They climbed down out of Tango One and headed over to Hangar Two.

On the way over, Peter stopped briefly to chat with one of the RAF Regiment Gunners, who was guarding the doors.

They might be in a rush, but some things are more important.

"At ease, Gunner." Peter addressed the guard,

"What's your name son?" he asked.

The RAF regiment Gunner was a tall, solidly built guy, who reminded Peter of his father. Stan had also been in the RAF regiment, and had stood guard outside countless aircraft hangars whilst the 'flyboys' swanned around. Peter had a great deal of time for the guys who kept them all safe.

"My name's Pete, Sir, but the lads all call me Peel, seeing as how I like oranges so much. Always have one in my pocket for emergencies. You never know when you might need a snack to keep your energy up."

Peter chuckled at the thought of an 'emergency orange'!

"Have you been in the service long, Gunner Peel?"

Now the guard chuckled to himself, at the thought of one of the top knobs calling him 'Gunner Peel'.

"A few years in, Sir. Long enough to remember a spot of bother we had here a few years back, when some wicked 'terrorists' stole the old Display Vulcan from under our noses. There was a right 'to do' about it, and everyone thought we'd get the boot. Strangely enough though, the brass decided that no action would be taken against anyone on duty that night and it all just 'went away'."

Peter scratched his chin, trying hard not to laugh. "I seem to recall something like that happening. I heard that the perpetrators were a proper rum bunch. Really bad characters..."

"I believe they were, Sir, I believe they were."

Peter could have sworn Gunner Peel winked at him, but surely he wouldn't be taking the Mickey out of one of the bosses...

Humph called over to Peter,

"Sorry to break into your cosy chat, but we are in somewhat of a rush..."

"I'll be with you in a second, I've just got something else I need to ask here."

Peter turned back to Gunner Peel.

"Pass me your notebook, Gunner, I've got a special order for you."

* * *

When Peter finally went through the door into Hangar Two, he saw the outline of another black Vulcan, only this time he didn't need any introduction.

"Hello there Zero One, I see that you've got one of the new paint jobs."

But somehow not quite the same as Tango One. This was not the same jet black. Peter could see some minor variations in the blackness, with some of the 'paint' looking more like just dark black, rather than deepest darkest black.

And then he realised what he was looking at.

"Bob, the old bird's got camouflage!"

"Yes, and to be honest, we're not really sure what caused it.

The best working theory goes like this; but don't ask me to explain the physics of it, because that's beyond any current understanding:

We think that it's due to the explosion at Bandar Abbas which, I'm sure you remember vividly, stripped off all the paint and fused the original rivets and panels together into one single piece of heat treated metal.

Before that, back when you first saw the silver coating, it had been added over the top of the original green and grey camouflage scheme.

It seems that those slight differences in thickness of paint, caused by the underlying camouflage scheme, were enough to produce tiny variations in the surface of the metal, at a molecular level. This was not visible when we repainted it silver, but once the graphene layer was added, these molecular variations started showing though, as a pattern in the level of absorption.

If you look really closely, you can even make out where the original RAF roundels were."

Peter could see on the wings, and by the side of the cockpit, that where the old red, white and blue roundels had been, there were definite circular variations in the level of blackness.

He remembered a story he'd been told of how the Vulcans got their distinctive camouflage scheme.

It was after a U2 spy plane had been shot down by a surface-to-air-missile, which meant that V-Force could now no longer rely on flying high and fast to stay safe.

They had to change tactics, and now they had to fly low and fast. Very low, below RADAR cover, and at those levels, very scarily fast.

It also meant that the white anti flash paint had to be changed to a camouflage scheme, and the task of finding a suitable camouflage design was allocated to a certain Wing Commander Woods...

... Who soon discovered that, of course, nothing suitable existed for a great big delta wing bomber... so he simply made one up himself.

Apparently he just drew a blotchy version of his initials A,E,G,W, backwards onto the outline of a Vulcan, and it was accepted as the pattern for the whole Vulcan fleet!

Peter looked up at Zero One, who appeared to have embraced this tradition, and had also decided to make up its own black and 'not quite black' design.

And it did look pretty impressive.

Without quite knowing why, Peter stood to attention by the side of his old friend, and raised his hand in an impromptu salute.

"Well played, Zero One. Very well played."

Chapter 7: Wingman

Humph interrupted Peter's 'moment' with Zero One.

"Bob can update you on all the technical upgrades he's made to your old Vulcan while you change into some flying gear, Peter.

As I said, we are on a very tight timeframe and you need to be in the air in 15 minutes. The ground crew have Zero One ready to go already.

Once you are in the air, I can update you on the next part of the mission, and Flight Lieutenant Kai Soong will tell you everything you need to know about orbital space flight and attitude adjustment. You'll need to take special notes on the latter, as I understand from your personnel file that you've never been very good at attitude adjustment!"

Peter's first thought was; that this was like being back on QRA - just 15 minutes to get airborne.

His second thought was; that Humph was a cheeky whatsit, telling him he had an attitude problem... although to be fair, he had a point...

His third thought was;

"And who exactly is Flt Lt Soong then?"

Humph took Peter by the elbow, and walked him towards a crew building at the side of the hangar.

"We will answer all your questions Peter, but you've got a couple of hours in the air ahead of you, so that can wait for the moment.

Let's just get you into the Vulcan as soon as possible."

* * *

Peter was changed into a full environmental suit and sitting in the cockpit of the Vulcan less than 12 minutes later; sitting at the end of the runway, where the aircraft had been towed out by the ground crew while he got suited and booted.

Bob had already updated Peter on the changes to Zero One, and had expected a trademark Barten explosion along the lines of:

"What the ruddy hell do you mean, you've taken away my turbojets, and replaced them with ruddy Roger Ramjets..." etc.

Instead, when Bob had hesitantly explained:

... How they had decided that instead of a hybrid airplane, with four turbojets and three HOTOL RB545 engines bolted on to the rear end, it made more sense to replace the turbojets with new engines developed by the same team that had created the SABRE engines used in Tango One...

... That they could repurpose the space saved by removing the RB545 engines...

... That the new engines were called Scimitars, capable of Mach 5 flight...

... That, in simple terms they were the 'air breathing' element of the SABRE engine design, developed as part of the EU funded Long term Advanced Propulsion Concepts and Technologies (LAPCAT) programme...

... Peter's only response was a trademark Barten bad joke:

"SABRE engines, Scimitar engines... you'll be telling me next you've added an engine to my old push-bike, and renamed it a flaming Raleigh Cutlass or something.

What is this, international speak like a pirate day... Yo Ho, me hearties!"

One of the ground crew was passing the open door at that point, and Peter heard him call out to the rest of his team.

"I reckon that new Navy rank has gone to the Black Commander's head, he thinks he's an effing pirate now boys...

Well, he may be Navy 'out there', but in here, I reckon we'll just use a proper old RAF term.

On this base we'll use Wing Commander, eh, call him a proper Wing Co and that..."

Peter heard one of the crew shout back, "Aye, Taff, we always knew that Barten was a proper Wing Co..."

Maybe it was the way he had pronounced the last couple of words that made the crew fall around laughing - that was the only thing Peter could think of.

Some things never changed between ground crew and the 'fly-boys'.

Peter had turned to Bob.

"Seriously though, mate, I've had enough experience with the HOTOL engines, and if you're telling me that this is the same technology, but upgraded and better, then that's fine with me.

It was Ray who was always the one who was averse to anything new..."

If Ray had been there, the resulting banter between Peter and Ray about who was actually the most scaredy-cat would have probably delayed the Vulcan take off so long that the Russian Cosmonauts would not only have run out of air, the ISS would have crashed into the surface of the Earth, the unsurvivable Black Death would be rampaging across the globe, humanity would be in terminal decline and the two of them would still be trying to get the last word in.

Instead, Peter was sat alone in the cockpit of a strangely quiet Zero One, talking to Black Control... with his imaginary pal sat in the back of the cabin...

"Battery on... engine start... now."

"New adventures, Ray... new adventures for the two of us..."

He hit the rapid start buttons, throttles forward, power rising, hand brake off... go... and he was moving within six seconds.

The runway sped under his wheels, and less than 15 minutes after Humph had taken his elbow, he was back in the air.

* * *

"Black Control to Zero One."

Peter recognised Humph's voice.

"Go ahead Black Control."

"Peter, we'll do away with the formalities again. Now you're en route I can give you a proper update - you aren't going to be doing much whilst the auto-pilot flies the plane, as we've already uploaded the flight plan, so hand over control now old chap and let the plane take the strain... Oh, and Peter, strap in, there are no constraints on this mission, so you will be supersonic about... now."

The sonic boom broke every window in Harmston, a little village unlucky enough to be under the flight path at just the wrong moment; but then, as Peter would have mulled to himself, if he'd known the carnage that he was unwittingly reaping once more upon an innocent Lincolnshire village, there are different levels of 'unlucky'.

As the auto-pilot levelled the Vulcan off at 90,000 feet, and the machometer went up rapidly until it settled at 5.5, Peter listened to Humph...

"Peter, you're in that seat because they tell me you're a pretty good pilot, that you have a cool head in an emergency situation, and most importantly, that you can think for yourself.

You are going to need all of that over the next couple of days.

They also tell me that you can sleep anywhere, so once I've briefed you, and Flt Lt Soong has gone over the concepts of flying in space with you, I suggest you take the chance to get some shut-eye. There isn't going to be a lot of opportunity for sleep now until this is over one way or another.

Currently you are on the way to the George Bush Intercontinental Airport in Houston, Texas. The Americans have declared an emergency and closed the airport, so you will be the only person using it today.

Once you arrive, they have an Osprey waiting to fly you out to the Johnson Space Centre. They have a team waiting at the Neutral Buoyancy Lab to take you through an accelerated Zero Gravity training program.

You should be floating about in the NBL in two hours, and their advice is that an hour and a half in the 'pool' and half an hour with some advanced trainers should be enough to prevent you making a complete idiot of yourself once you are up in orbit. Everything clear so far, Peter?"

Peter's head was spinning, and it wasn't the Mach number or the after effects of yesterday's beer-fest... Was that only a few hours ago?..

And then he thought about the two blokes trapped in the ISS, not knowing if anyone was coming to help, and only too aware that they were using up their air supply all too quickly...

"All clear, Humph. What else do I need to know?"

Humph smiled to himself. Some of the 'suits' had told him not to use Peter and the UN planes, that this needed a purely military response, but his gut had told him that he should go with this plan. Like all good leaders, he knew you couldn't quantify the accuracy of a gut response, but in a crisis, and by God, this was a crisis, it was all you could trust.

"Good man, Peter. I'm handing over to Flt Lt Soong for the rest of the briefing. He knows more about flying a plane in orbital mode than anyone else on the planet, so do take his advice. Also, you're going to be working together pretty closely from now on, so try to be nice!"

* * *

"Black Control to Zero One. This is Flight Lieutenant Soong for Commander Barten. Do you read me?"

"Zero One to Black Control. I read you loud and clear. Nice radio protocol Flight Lieutenant Soong.

Very old school, the old Air Electronics Officer in me appreciates it,

But if the Air Vice-Marshal and I can dispense with formalities, then I'm sure the two of us can. Just call me Peter. Do you mind if I call you Kai?"

Peter was 'being nice'.

"Yes, Peter. That will be acceptable. Can I ask, how much do you know about Spacecraft Attitude Control, specifically three axis stabilisation using small thrusters?"

Peter's reply was short and sweet, well not so sweet. He looked around, ready to throw a couple of coins into Ray's famous swear box; the little plastic jar which he had screwed onto the rear nav table to stop others pinching it.

Oh, well, I saved a couple of quid there, he thought to himself when he realised there was no nav table, never mind a swear box.

"Sorry, Kai, I should have said 'not very much'."

"Your reply was not a problem for me, and given the levels of tension relating to this mission, a certain amount of profanity to relieve the pressure is completely natural, Peter.

Now, please allow me to explain the principals of thruster control, but before that, I should probably touch on the basic concepts of Attitude Determination. I think that due to the time constraints of this mission, you won't really have the opportunity to attain a full understanding of the Attitude Control Algorithms, but it will be important for me at least explain some of the underlying theories..."

If Peter expected he was going to have a nice quiet rest whilst the auto-pilot did the work on this trip, he was wrong.

If he thought his head had been spinning before, he was wrong again.

* * *

After an hour of 'professional development', Peter finally decided that his brain was at saturation point.

"Kai, I think I've got the gist of it, and to be honest, the last few things you just said to me went straight in one ear and out the other. As we're going to be working pretty closely over the next couple of days, we should probably get to know a little bit about each other, don't you think?"

Kai replied,

"You are correct that it will be important for us to understand each other's motivations, if we are to function as a fully coherent unit over the next 81 hours, so I agree that we should spend the next 30 minutes exploring each other's character and motivations..."

Peter sighed to himself quietly... this was going to be very different to a bit of banter with Ray.

"Kai, if you don't mind me saying, you have a very distinct way of speaking, but it sounds strangely familiar to me. Have we met before?"

"Peter, I can categorically state that we have never met before, but I can tell from accessing your records that you will definitely recognise my voice pattern. It is based on the character of Data, and I can see that Star Trek, The Next Generation is one of your favourite TV shows."

"You're putting on a voice? I don't understand."

Now this is getting weird, thought Peter.

"No, this is the voice assigned to me. Peter, I thought you understood, I am a Quantum Artificial Intelligence - QAI.

You have probably heard of the Collaborative Combat Aircraft, or 'Drone Wingman' projects. I am a step development on from that. I am effectively the whole of Tango Two, with a quantum 'brain' and free thinking AI.

In Star trek lore, you could say I am the equivalent to Data, with a Positronic brain, although I don't have a physical presence – well, except for being a Space Plane I suppose..."

Peter's jaw was on the floor again.

This was getting weirder by the moment, but he decided to go with the flow.

"Qai, did you just make a joke?"

"Ha. I tried Peter, I appreciate that you noticed. It's a new skill that I am attempting to acquire. Having studied your interactions with other colleagues, I recognised that it is the fundamental driving factor in most of your conversations." replied Qai.

Peter was self aware enough to accept that most of his interactions with 'the team' were jokey - not all the time, just enough to keep him sane. But sometimes you had to be serious.

"Qai, you said 'Tango Two'. I was only shown Tango One back at Black Station. Has Zero One been redesignated as Tango Two?"

"No, Peter, your aircraft is still Zero One. There wasn't time for you to see everything before. Tango Two and its bold captain are currently housed in Hangar Three. Come in and say hello when you get back."

"I will, Qai, but tell me a little bit more about yourself, other than the whole 'being a space plane' thing. I have to say that there is a superb irony in having spent the last hour being briefed about how to fly in space, by an actual space plane, who is in fact based on a Star Trek character..."

"Hmm," Qai mused, "there is an irony in that, and I think I will need to reflect on what you said about me being 'based on a Star Trek character'.

I believe that one of the development team at Department 'T' was what you would call a 'Nerd', and I am starting to think that he may have infused a bit too much of his own character into my coding."

"What's Department 'T', Qai, I've never heard of that before." Peter asked.

"It's formally called the Turing Project, set up along the lines of the Manhattan Project, to develop an AI personality that is completely indistinguishable from a human personality.

For some reason everyone calls it Department T. Apparently that is a joke, but I am yet to understand the humour. People phone the project and ask for someone called Vic, and whoever is in the office at the time has to answer 'I think you called the wrong number, I'll put you through to Department S'. Then everyone laughs."

Peter snorted.

"So it is funny, Peter, but I don't understand. A scientist called Victor ended up under investigation. They said that he must have told people that he worked in Department S, and they did not believe that he had not told anybody, because so many people called up to ask if he was there."

Peter cracked up.

"Qai, you might have a positronic brain or whatever, but remind me never to enter a pub quiz with you. Do me a favour and look up a band called 'Department S' will you."

After a second, Qai answered.

"Oh, I see. I think I will have to work a bit more on the science of 'jokes'. I obviously still have a lot to learn."

Peter was nearly crying with laughter.

"You're OK. Believe me, you're a pretty funny guy, Qai."

And then Peter lost it completely.

Chapter 8. Neutral Buoyancy

"George Bush Intercontinental to Zero One. We have airspace and airport clear for your arrival. Do we have permission to upload a flight plan to your autopilot, for the approach to runway one?

We have an aircraft on standby, ready to transport you directly to the Johnson Space Centre."

"Zero One to George Bush. Please go ahead and send the data for the autopilot.

I'm getting pretty used to just sitting in the old captain's chair, and letting the plane do the flying...

It's about time I put in for my retirement. Time to get out before they make the bloke in the pilot's seat completely redundant."

"Black Control to Zero One. Peter, It's Humph here. If I were you I'd let the plane take the strain as much as possible for the moment, and save your flying brain for the mission itself. Believe me, you're going to need it. We have a plan in place for your next steps, after the training has completed at the Space Centre. You won't be coming directly back to Black Station, there's some rather important kit to pick up on the way, so there'll be a slight diversion. Qai has the details, and will brief you once you're on the flight back."

"OK, Humph, I'll be a good boy and do as I'm told. Plane taking strain. Pilot engaging eyelid resting mode for the next quarter of an hour..."

* * *

Fifteen minutes later, the intercom buzzed back into life.

"George Bush Intercontinental to Zero One. Can you confirm that you are on approach?"

Peter disengaged eyelid resting mode. A shame really, as he had just been reliving a spot of serious bird watching that had taken place a few years back in a little dacha to the south of Moscow, with his friend Ivan.

To be honest, not a great deal of ornithology went on, just a lot of talk, and even that petered out as the stock of 'Russian medicine' was depleted.

He checked that the auto pilot had engaged, and that the Vulcan was actually in the descent path before replying.

"Zero One to George Bush. Confirmed. On approach as planned."

The Vulcan slid down the glide path towards the touchdown point and greased onto the runway with the minimum of effort. It rolled gently down the full length and stopped at the far end without even rocking the nose downwards as the brakes applied.

"George Bush Intercontinental to Zero One. There is no need to taxi, we are coming to you. We will refuel and turn the aircraft around at the end of the runway, so you are ready for immediate take off when you require it. Advise you stay in the cabin for the moment."

Peter heard what sounded like turboprop engines, but these were right on top of him!

He looked out the cockpit window and saw what appeared to be a plane, but with its engines pointing perpendicular to the wings. It was landing vertically only a few yards away from the Vulcan.

Seconds after landing, four Marines jumped from the loading ramp at the back of the aircraft and sprinted over to the Vulcan.

"George Bush Intercontinental to Zero One. Commander Barten, please exit now and we will escort you to your ride. The Marines have orders to guard Zero One until you return. Safe travels."

Peter climbed down from the cockpit, and was surprised when the Marines snapped to attention and saluted him. One of them stepped forward.

"Sir, we have orders to escort you to Tango Osprey. At the order of the President of the United States of America, it is now transferred to your command."

The Marines took Peter over to the loading ramp and handed him over to the aircrew like a piece of precious cargo. They saluted him again and sprinted back to the Vulcan to set up a perimeter; one stood on guard at the front of the aircraft, one at each wingtip and one at the rear. Peter looked over towards the airport terminal, and saw more Marines racing towards the Vulcan.

The pilot of the Osprey beckoned Peter over.

"Strap in Commander, we're taking off, and I'll close the tailgate ramp as we go. Don't want you falling out... Someone around here obviously thinks you're important."

Peter laughed.

"I was starting to take myself seriously there. What's with all the security?"

"Oh, that's just standard operating procedure. The President has given you the same security status as a visiting Head of State. Like I said, someone thinks you're important. Technically you're now in command of this aircraft, but if you don't mind, I'll take it from here."

They were already in the air - undertaking a vertical takeoff that was transitioning in front of Peter's eyes into horizontal flight, as the engines swivelled away from pointing upwards, down to become forward facing turboprops, and the aircraft accelerated rapidly.

The pilot could see Peter taking it all in like a schoolboy.

"It's impressive when you see it for the first time isn't it Commander?"

"I've seen some things, but not one of these before. And call me Peter. I prefer things a bit more informal."

"Sure thing, Peter. My names Hank. We're all pilots here. This beauty is the Bell Boeing V-22 Osprey. I can do a vertical takeoff and landing or a short takeoff and landing, depending on how much I tilt the engine nacelles. Or of course, I could just leave them horizontal, and then this is just a 'normal' fixed wing aircraft. Same as any old aircraft.

It's technically a third type of aircraft design, neither a fixed wing or a helicopter - it's called a 'Tiltrotor'. As you just saw, it can operate as a helicopter with the nacelles vertical and rotors horizontal. Then once airborne, those old nacelles just rotate forward 90° for horizontal flight, converting the V-22 into a more fuel-efficient, higher-speed aircraft. Like I said, same as any old turboprop aircraft.

The President put this one at your command, as it's the fastest way to get you back and forth between George Bush Intercontinental and the Johnson Space Centre. Unless you have any other orders, once I get you down onto the ground at the JSC, we'll just order in some coffees, and wait to jump you back to your Vulcan.

You can see the JSC ahead of us. If you look about 6 miles northwest of the JSC you can see some landing strips. They're right next to the Neutral Buoyancy Lab. We'll be landing there in a couple of minutes.

If it's Ok with you we'll exit you out the back door - it's quicker, but don't worry, I'll try to make sure we're actually on the ground before the crew push you out."

Peter chuckled.

Well he had said he liked it informal... he couldn't imagine Hank normally joked about pushing 'Heads of State' off a loading ramp, whilst the aircraft was still in the air. Although he could think of a few that would definitely benefit from the experience!

"My thanks, your concern for my safety is duly noted. Out of gratitude, and as your current commander, which was decreed by the President himself, I think I should override your suggestion of ordering in coffees, and replace said coffees with 'proper' English breakfast tea instead. Just like my old mum used to brew, the tea bag making just the briefest contact with lukewarm water, before adding evaporated milk and two spoons of sugar to make it vaguely drinkable. Lovely stuff... you could even order a couple of rich tea biscuits to complete the experience."

He didn't wait to hear the response, but guessed that Hank framed it in suitable aircrew language.

* * *

There was a jeep waiting for Peter when he jumped down from the back of Tango Osprey.

There was more saluting, and Peter could see Hank's grin as he sat in the cockpit, no doubt ordering the coffees already...

Then he was bouncing around in the passenger seat of a jeep as it sped away from the Osprey, towards a big white building, and he could feel his teeth banging together with every jolt.

Peter thought to himself. "I know there's a time pressure, but does everything have to be done at a hundred miles an hour, surely they could spare a thought for my old bones..."

Before he'd even finished the thought, the jeep had screeched to a stop, and there was another welcoming committee waiting for him.

"Good Morning Commander Barten. My name is Major Edward Green, United States Space Force. I will be your liaison officer while you are with us. I have already been briefed that you prefer an informal command structure.. so I guess, Hi, I'm Ted."

Peter decided it was time for a bit of fun.

"Major Green, I have no idea how you behave in your Space Force, but a senior member of the British Armed Forces cannot, and will not, accept that level of impertinence. I assure you that I expect nothing less than the respect my rank demands."

He could see Ted going pale in front of him. Peter continued,

"I think you should commence some formal grovelling, with added obsequious deference and a large amount of general purpose boot-licking... at the double." He winked, "Or you could just call me Peter."

Ted breathed again.

"Yeah, they also briefed me that you liked a joke, but for a second there I thought you were serious.

Let me walk you through to the training centre. They are just going to take you through the basics of manoeuvring during extravehicular activities, and let you get some hands-on time with mock-ups of the equipment we are sending back with you. It's being loaded into your Vulcan as we speak.

Sorry for the rush, but as you only have an hour and a half scheduled here, we need you in the pool straight away.

Peter had undertaken sea survival training with the RAF, and enjoyed a spot of canoeing, so he had thought that he was relatively comfortable in the water.

The next hour and a half was like nothing he'd ever known. He was thrust into an EVA suit, which was possibly the most uncomfortable thing he had ever experienced, and then he was expected to undertake precise control operations, with equipment that he had never seen before, in a neutral buoyancy environment which simulated the weightlessness of space.

Eventually, all his senses were befuddled, and when they finally pulled him out, he felt less prepared than before he got anywhere near the Johnson Space Centre.

"Ted, that was a complete waste of time. I hate to say it, but there's no way I will be able to complete this mission. They need to send up someone who actually knows what they're doing in space."

"Peter, we knew that this was never going to be enough training. There's just isn't the time.

But there isn't anyone else. You're it.

You need to meet someone else. I'm taking you to meet your advanced trainer."

* * *

Once again Peter was in the passenger seat of the jeep. This time with Ted at the wheel, and if anything, they were going faster. It was less bumpy though, as they were speeding through the streets instead of across an airfield.

"Don't you have speed limits, Ted?" he asked.

"We do. But apparently you don't Peter. I was told to put my foot down… traffic control have fixed the lights so we get green lit straight through, and the traffic police are keeping everyone out of our way."

"I thought the roads were clear - I just put that down to the time of day." replied Peter. "Although, to be honest, I have no idea what time of day it is here."

He looked down at his watch, which was still set to GMT.

"12:30 in the UK, so what does that make it here in Houston?"

"It's 06:30 Peter, just coming up to what would normally be rush hour."

"Ah, time for breakfast then," said Peter, suddenly feeling hungry.

"Funny you should say that," said Ted, taking a sudden turn, after passing a billboard that read, 'Welcome to the Outpost Tavern.'

Chapter 9. Building 99

The jeep pulled up in front of what could best be described as a beaten up dive bar.

Ted jumped out the driver's seat with a massive grin on his face.

"The sign might say Welcome to the Outpost Tavern, but at NASA, we call this building 99. It's where all the real work gets done. Let's get some breakfast, and you can meet Frank.

How do Brits feel about beer with their breakfast, Peter?"

"Well, normally I just have a nice cuppa, but if you're offering, it would be rude not to, and besides," he looked down at his watch again, "according to my trusty time-piece, the sun's already up over the yardarm, so it would not just be rude, I'd probably be in breach of Navy regulations if we didn't have a glass or two."

Ted laughed, "You seem to be taking your new navy rank very seriously now, Peter, but I don't think we should have more than one.

You've got to fly back across the Atlantic in less than an hour, and I don't want to get the blame if you fall asleep and end up landing in the Falklands or somewhere."

"You're right, Ted, I don't want to be back down in that neck of the woods again... but there's no risk of getting lost, that Vulcan will pretty much fly itself these days. I'm simply a passenger, one who just happens to be sitting in the captain's chair."

Ted was having nothing of Peter's new found despondency about his level of 'un' importance,

"Peter, I want to read you something from your personnel record - well at least the section we have been sent - apparently, some information is too highly classified for even NASA to know.

Do you recognise these words?

'As far as I'm concerned the computers could get on with it, but I will make sure that they are correct. The artificial intelligence of these "brains" is not yet at the stage where the fear and the sheer panic of a possible collision in mid air, with its impending doom, would make a computer grip the control stick and pull like hell to get out of the way of a hundred tons of metal coming towards me at a combined speed of a couple of thousand miles per hour. That simple pleasure could be left to the human being at the sharp end.

I will trust the computers only so far, because where my skin is involved, I'm the one who will make sure it stays in one piece...'

I believe someone called Peter Barten uttered those words of wisdom."

Peter was stunned.

"How the heck do you have that. I remember thinking something like that when we were meeting up with Michel's enormous Tupolev TU-20 Bear, and I was worried about the computers pointing us towards each other on the same flight path, but I never wrote it up in a report. Don't tell me 'they' can read minds now, because if they can, I'm in real trouble..."

Ted pushed open the saloon bar doors and walked into 'building 99', and said,

"No, Peter, nothing as sinister as that. Did nobody ever tell you that you have a habit of speaking your thoughts out loud. You obviously don't even know you're doing it. The cockpit voice recorder picked it up, and it gets transcribed after each mission. Let's just say that 'they' don't need to read your mind... you tell them yourself..."

Peter went pale, while he recalled all the 'thoughts' he'd ever said to himself in the cockpit of Zero One...

"Oh, for chuffing chuff's sake. I'm toast..." and then, "I guess that will be what's in the 'super highly classified' section of my records then!"

* * *

Ted walked Peter up to the bar, and introduced him to the barman.

"Frank, this is Peter, the reluctant astronaut we discussed. He needs some traditional NASA hospitality, and more than anything, he desperately needs to hear some of your advanced astronaut strategies. The poor guy just spent an hour and a half in the pool, and now thinks he hasn't got the Right Stuff."

Ted turned to Peter.

"I don't have time to stay for breakfast - I have to check that everything has been loaded up onto your Vulcan, and I'll make sure it's ready to go once you are finished here. I'll come back to pick you up, but Frank here will look after you. He might look like a scruffy barman, but Frank Carven is NASA's most experienced astronaut. He bought this place after he retired, and spends his days imparting words of wisdom to all the new trainee astronauts."

He nodded his head over to a group of four clean cut Tom Cruise clones, sat at a table with some young ladies, who appeared to be hanging onto every word of their daring astronaut exploits.

"None of them will listen to him though, they think they know it all already...

... But I thought an old hand like you would appreciate his advice.

See you later."

Frank smiled at Ted as he left the tavern.

"He's a good lad, makes me proud every day. Got a cheek though, calling us old...

Let me get you some Outpost Home Fries and a drink, then we can have a chat. Take a stool at the bar, Peter. I'll be back in a minute."

Peter looked around the bar, and took a moment to relax after the frenzy of activity that had swept him up since he'd had his meeting with Guy and Humph out the back of the Brewer.

Looking around the Outpost, he thought that it wasn't that different to the Brewer.

Instead of the big 'Hiawatha', the Brewer's totem pole that had been carved out of six feet of solid pine trunk, which sat in pride of place near the fire, the Outpost had its own 'totem'; a six foot scale model of a Saturn 5 rocket at the end of the bar.

Where the Brewer had a refurbished jukebox that churned out the oldies, the Outpost had what looked like an original vintage Wurlitzer, and it too was playing the 'oldies'.

At that exact moment in time, Peter was once again listening to Mr Sinatra's dulcet tones inviting him to 'Fly me to the moon...'

Peter couldn't help but chuckle to himself. "Let's hope he gets to the end of the song this time!"

Frank placed a plate in front of Peter, a bottle of beer at the right of the plate, and a bottle of ketchup at the left. The plate was loaded with cubed potatoes, mixed together with chopped peppers and onions.

"Best home fries you'll taste. It's an old family recipe, except I add a bit of smoked paprika to give it a slight punch. With Brooklyn beer to wash it down.

My family came from Brooklyn, so I like to keep up the tradition.

You eat up, Peter.

I saw you looking around the place, I hope you like it. I had to rebuild it from the ground up. The old place closed down and was taken over; they turned it into a TexMex, and then let it burn down when it wasn't making enough money.

So when I retired I bought the empty lot, and we rebuilt the old Tavern back to how it was supposed to be. Believe it or not, this place is only a few years old, except for the Wurlitzer, that's an original."

Peter didn't take long to finish his 'breakfast'. He hadn't realized how hungry he was until the food was in front of him. He supped his beer, and asked,

"Frank, I know Ted thinks you can talk some sense into me, but I just don't see how I can pull this mission off. I know my way around a plane, but how am I supposed to manoeuvre around in space after just a few hours of training?"

Frank looked into Peter's eyes, and didn't say anything for a good three minutes. Peter could sense Frank 'inspecting' him, and waited for him to speak.

"You'll have heard the phrase 'The Right Stuff'; Ted mentioned it earlier. Well that's not just a bunch of words. It's what keeps you alive in space.

There's another phrase you won't know.

'Five percent training, five percent fear, and ninety percent adrenaline'.

That's what kept me alive in space.

Forget the training in the pool. That was just so that the first time you experienced the suit, the equipment, and the weightlessness, it wouldn't be when you're actually up there.

Think of it as aversion therapy. It's to get you used to the fear of what you don't know. Only idiots like those boys over there don't get scared - because they think they know it all.

I can tell you now that not one of them has the right stuff. They'll all get booted off the training in less than a month.

Ted told me about you, Peter, and you have instincts.

The pool was to train your instincts, so that when the adrenaline kicks in, you'll know what to do.

If you don't, then a lot of people are going to be dead, and from what I see in you, you're not about to let that happen."

He let Peter think about that for a second, and then;

"Peter, have you seen the film 'The Martian'. There's a bit where Matt Damon gives the most important bit of advice for surviving in space. I try to tell it to all the young guns over there, but they just think I'm a crazy old coot."

Peter answered, "Do you mean the bit where he says something about solving one problem and then the next, and if you solve enough problems, you can get home?"

Frank laughed, "No, everyone thinks it's that bit. But all he's saying there is that if you solve the all the problems you'll be OK. Well duh!

That doesn't give you any practical, down to earth advice. Listen carefully to what I say next, Peter, because this is the goods. This is what you need to know to save a life in space..."

And then Frank put on his best Matt Damon voice:

"Yes, of course duct tape works in a near-vacuum. Duct tape works anywhere. Duct tape is magic and should be worshipped.

We gave them that line, Peter, when they were researching for the film.

Truest words ever spoken."

* * *

With his final words of wisdom imparted, Frank winked at Peter and wandered over to a different section of the bar, to serve a couple of customers who had just walked in.

Peter rolled the beer bottle around in his hand, and thought about what Frank had said:

He was right about duct tape. You could ask any of the ground crew back in the hangars at Black Station, and to a man they would swear to its magical powers.

He was also right about Peter.

When the proverbial hit the fan, and in every mission, it always did, then it wasn't what someone told you in a training session that saved the day. It was the person in the hot seat, relying on their instincts. Sometimes it didn't matter if you did the 'right thing', you just had to do something, and hope it worked out. If you over thought it, then it was already too late.

Ted and Frank were telling him the same thing that Guy and Humph had been saying.

Peter was the one that needed to complete the mission, because he was the one in the hot seat. They could have chosen someone else, but they hadn't. For whatever reason, the stars had aligned and Peter Barten was the one that needed to fly around in zero gravity and save the world...

Well, so be it.

He looked down at his beer, and saw a bowl of snacks on the bar that he hadn't noticed before.

PopNuts. A mixture of what looked like salted peanuts and popcorn.

Even though he'd just finished off a plate of home fries, he grabbed a handful and shovelled them into his mouth.

Not bad, he thought, and washed them down with the last of his beer.

Ted will be back to pick me up soon, he thought, and then back to Blighty, looking out for the cathedral as I fly past Lincoln.

Lincoln Cathedral, George Bush Intercontinental, Johnson Space Centre.

Ha, he thought to himself. What a day... visiting a trio of ex Presidents, given a 'Tiltrotor' on loan from the current POTUS, and the day is still young.

Life could be a lot worse...

* * *

"Just listen to the crazy old limey at the bar, talking to himself about our presidents. What a nut job!"

It was one of the Tom Cruise clones, and Peter suddenly realised he must have been speaking his thoughts out loud again.

That was something he really needed to get a grip on, before it got him into trouble.

But for the moment, someone else was going to have a spot of trouble.

His famous inability to put up with young 'oiks' temporarily got the better of him, and unfortunately there was nobody around him to talk sense, so...

Peter stepped away from his stool, marched over to the group, and...

"Would you care to repeat that to my face, or are you going to hide behind these young 'dolly birds'.

And I'm not referring to the young ladies in your company."

One of the 'young guns' stood up... and up... and up...

He must have been over 6'6'', and now Peter could get a proper look, he was also built like a brick house.

Peter's next thought was, "Barten, you're an eejit..."

Then all those years of close combat training, all the aggression techniques kindly passed on to him by his SAS 'instructors' in the Brecon Beacons when he was on Evasion and Escape training, to prepare him for an 'unplanned landing' behind enemy lines; it all now culminated in Peter's next instinctive thoughts and actions...

"Go for the soft parts."

Peter placed an expertly aimed knee to the young gun's groin, and as the latter crumpled to the floor, letting out a pitiful, pained groan of abject misery, he turned and walked back to his bar stool, suddenly feeling a lot better with himself.

For approximately ten seconds...

He felt someone grab the back of his head, and the next sensation he had was his mouth, nose and eyes full of popcorn and salty peanuts as they carefully positioned him face down in the bowl of snacks...

Once again, he was pinned down in a pub, this time being held down onto the bar top, locked solid and unable to move a muscle.

Once again their hands were the size of dinner plates...

"Barten, you're not just an eejit, you're a chuffing eejit. You never weigh up the odds properly. No wonder you always lose at cards. Even a novice gambler knows that the 'house' stacks the odds against you, and this is their home turf..."

A voice spoke menacingly into his ear.

"So you think we're a bunch of dolly birds do you? We don't think that's very polite. We think you're gonna need a little education..."

Peter felt his head being pulled back up, and the next thing he saw was the bunched up fist of a different 'young gun', two inches from his nose, travelling fast in the direction of his face.

The next thing he heard was;

"Do you need a bit of a hand over there, Mr Barten?"

Peter looked over at the saloon door, and standing there was Hulk One, with his compatriot Hulk Two next to him, both grinning like Cheshire Cats.

Before he could answer, they had arrived at the bar, peeled the young gun's hand off the back of his head, and propelled Peter forcibly in the direction of the door.

Peter fell through the door, and landed face first in the dust.

"They asked us to escort you, for your 'personal protection' - given that you have such a talent for finding trouble.

They didn't tell you, because they thought you might refuse to have us around. I can't think why.

Apparently it's important to someone that you get back to your Vulcan in one piece.

Speaking of which, that space at the rear of the plane, where we were unceremoniously shoved into before you took off - they said it's designed for special forces, so they can jump out the back instead of taking up space in your precious cabin. Anyway, it's now full up with NASA equipment, so if it's alright with you, we'll make our own way back home. After we finish up here that is..."

As they turned around to go back into the Outpost Tavern, Peter heard Ted's voice.

"I think we should get you on your way, Peter. I picked up your two friends when I borrowed the Osprey to ferry the kit over to your plane. The pilot was very put out that I interrupted his coffee, but I said I was acting on your direct orders, so you'd better back me up if he complains. Those two are a couple of interesting specimens, aren't they?

One of them left a parcel for you in the jeep. He said you would need it."

On the passenger seat, Peter saw a brown paper parcel, tied up with string.

He opened it, and inside was a piece of prime steak, and a note.

"For your face - to reduce the prospect of a shiner."

Very funny, thought Peter, but he still placed it over his left eye, the one that had taken the impact of a bunched fist a few minutes ago.

"Hang on, how did they know I was going to take a punch to the face... and how long had they been stood at the door before they decided to involve themselves in my spot of bother?"

No wonder they had been grinning like Cheshire Cats... and they were supposed to be on his side!

He caught sight of himself in the mirror, his hair full of sticky popcorn and salted peanuts, a steak fixed over one eye, like a crazy pirate's eye patch, and couldn't help himself. He laughed so hard he cried, and that made his eye sting, which just made him laugh more...

"Something funny, Peter?" asked Ted.

"Yes, I was just thinking about that model Saturn 5, and the Wurlitzer. If past experience of my two friends is anything to go by, I suspect that said rocket is likely to be heading on a very precise trajectory into the complex inner workings of said juke box right about now."

Poor old Frank. He'd only just had the Outpost Tavern rebuilt.

You didn't have to be a gambling man to work out the odds of it needing another complete refurbishment in the not too distant future.

In fact, you wouldn't get 'evens' on that.

It was a guaranteed certainty!

Chapter 10. Crew Mates

Another fast, clear run back to the Osprey, and Peter was saying goodbye to Ted before being taken back to Zero One.

Ted caught his hold of his elbow.

"Peter, you've got company on the way back to George Bush. Someone who very much wanted to speak with you before your mission. I think you'll want to hear what she has to say.

Oh, and you take care of yourself up there.

Do you know something Peter, I'm jealous. If I could swap places with you, I'd go in an instant. You're about to do something that no man has done before, and see something that we can only hope that nobody ever has to see again. This is the stuff of history."

Peter looked back at Ted, and winked.

"Thanks for that, no pressure then...

Let's hope the history books don't record that Peter Barten went into space, and made a complete ass of himself!"

Ted walked to the loading ramp of the Osprey, and pointed towards the cockpit.

There was a different pilot sat at the controls.

"Hank's gone for an extended coffee break. Chief Astronaut Wilson will fly you to your Vulcan.

She requested an opportunity to meet with you.

She's not just an Osprey pilot..

... Less than 35 hours ago she led the evacuation, as Commander of the International Space Station."

* * *

As Peter strapped in, his new pilot looked at him intently. She appeared to be scrutinising him, as if he was a specimen on a microscope slide.

Peter marvelled once again as the Osprey soared vertically and transitioned into horizontal flight in just a few seconds.

"This is an amazing machine. It seems a shame I have to hand it back to the President when I leave. You don't think he'd let me keep it as a souvenir do you?"

She laughed, "You can ask him, but at over one hundred million dollars per aircraft, I think the Pentagon would have something to say about that."

"Maybe I'll leave it then. I wouldn't want to get him into trouble..." then, "Ted said you asked to speak with me?"

"Yes Peter. Let me introduce myself properly. My name is Peggy Wilson, and as Ted just told you, I was the commander of the ISS when it exploded. I had to order the evacuation, and abandon two of my crew mates.

I had to look into their faces as they watched us leave. I haven't slept since we left, but when I close my eyes, I see the look in their eyes as they realise we can't get them out, and it's haunting me.

I wanted to meet the person who is going to try to get them back.

If it's Ok with you, I wanted you to know who they are, and not just think of them as the two trapped cosmonauts..."

Peter put a hand on Peggy's arm, and said gently, "Please, tell me about your friends, I'd like to get to know them."

"Thank you Peter, I wasn't sure you would want to hear me out. Some people like to stay detached for a mission."

"That would have been me not too long ago," Peter replied, "but I've learnt some things about myself recently, and I think I need to know some more about these two men."

"They're both wonderful and crazy, Peter. And from what I've heard about you, crazy is not a bad thing.

We don't have long before we get to George Bush Intercontinental, so let me give you the quick version.

Alexander Grevenkin is from Saint Petersburg, ex Russian Air Force. He has a beautiful wife and two beautiful daughters, and he's in love with American Football. He claims that he's the Dallas Cowboys biggest fan, and everyone calls him Lexi.

Kyrylo Kadeniuk is from Odesa, he's a scientist. He worked with me in the Bio Lab. I'm also a scientist - a professor of biochemistry to be precise, and Kyri and I became close friends.

Very close friends, Peter. We were planning a life together after the mission completed..."

Peter couldn't see Peggy's eyes behind the NASA standard issue Aviator sunglasses, but he could hear the catch in her voice, and knew the tears were there.

"Peggy, I promise, I'll do everything in my power to bring them back."

She turned her head to stare at him again.

"No, Peter, that's not why I asked to meet with you. Kyri and I worked in the Bio Lab. You know what that means. We developed the Streptococcus-Yersinia hybrid, and we understood the danger.

Listen to me very carefully.

You don't do anything that will compromise the main mission.

If it's too difficult to get to Lexi and Kyri, you leave them.

The stakes are too high.

You launch the nuclear device, and you destroy the ISS.

You vaporise the threat of the Black Death....

And the man I love..."

Peter could see the tears now, streaming down her cheeks from behind the Aviators.

Chapter 11. Middle Game Theory

Four minutes later, Peter had jumped off the loading ramp at the back of 'his' Osprey, and watched as Peggy flew it back in the direction of the Johnson Space Centre.

Just before she took off, Peggy had also jumped out the back of the Osprey, and held out her sunglasses to him.

"Here, take these as a souvenir.

Looking at the state of your face, you're going to need something to hide a black eye real soon.

You remember what I said."

He put on his new Aviators, mentally said goodbye, and thought,

"That's what you call heroic. She's a hell of a brave woman."

Then he looked around to see if anyone had heard his thoughts. None of the Marines had reacted, so he guessed he hadn't said those particular thoughts out loud.

Got to keep a watch on that, he said to himself.

"Got to keep a watch on what, Sir?" asked one of the Marines, "and you're right about Chief Astronaut Wilson, Sir.

She is the bravest of the brave."

Peter put his hand over his mouth as he walked to the back of the Vulcan, to make sure his latest thoughts didn't escape on their own.

There wasn't a swear box big enough for that fine.

He inspected the new back end of Zero One, to take in the modifications that Bob had explained somewhat briefly back in Hangar Two. He'd mentioned that the rear of the aircraft had been repurposed, when they removed the three HOTOL RB545 engines and their fuel tanks, and now Peter could fully take in the changes.

The rear of the Vulcan had been rebuilt to match the smooth outline of the rest of the aircraft: it was the deep jet black of Tango One, since the metal used in the refurbishment hadn't been heat-treated courtesy of a thermonuclear explosion, so the new section didn't have the 'camouflage' scheme that decorated the rest of the plane.

He could just make out a line in the blackness that indicated where the tail end opened up, like the landing ramp at the rear of the Osprey, but smaller. That's where the ground crew could load cargo - as they had been doing with the NASA equipment, or where a black clad special services team could make a quick exit.

Peter chuckled to himself,

"It's a shame I didn't know Hulks One and Two were hitching a ride. I could have opened the back door at 90,000 feet, and made life very uncomfortable for them..."

He looked again at the black and not-so-black camo effect of the rest of the plane, and suddenly realised what he was seeing.

Like most boys, when he was little, he had collected bugs in jam jars, and he loved to read about different types of creepy-crawlies.

Moths were his favourite. Not butterflies, they were too pretty. He liked moths, and one in particular.

The Rustic Sphinx.

He never really knew why that was his favourite - perhaps it was just the name, but now, looking at the variegations in tone on the black surface of the Vulcan he realised;

"Zero One. You look like one great big Rustic Sphinx Moth. When we get back home, I'm going to ask the ground crew to paint 'Rusty' on the inside of your bomb bay doors, and we'll never let on to Bob why. It'll drive him crazy checking for rust damage..."

* * *

Three minutes later and he was suited and booted in the cockpit.

"George Bush Intercontinental to Zero One. Your flight plan back to the UK has been uploaded, runway one is open and the airspace is clear for your departure.

Safe travels, and good luck Commander Barten."

Peter engaged the autopilot, keeping a watch on the controls in case he had to take over during takeoff, but otherwise sat back and let the system do the work.

"Letting the plane take the strain. Peter Barten supervising, ensuring everything does what it's supposed to do."

Then he remembered that the cockpit voice recorder would be transcribed at the end of the mission.

"You just keep recording boys, and try to explain this transcription to your bosses..."

What followed would make a sailor blush, and Peter was again glad that Ray's swear box hadn't survived the refurbishment...

"Black Control to Zero One. This is Flight Lieutenant Soong for Commander Barten. Reading you loud and clear, but I'm afraid I didn't understand your last instruction.

Even if that was physically possible, why would anyone attempt to undertake such a feat. That sounds as if it would cause serious damage to more than one part of normal human physiology, and I'm sure it's illegal in most jurisdictions."

Peter laughed,

"I don't know if that was meant to be another joke, but like a said before, you're funny Qai."

"I am trying to be, Peter. I ran through some iterations after our last conversation. I believe I have improved.

I have been thinking about what you said, and working through some other aspects of my character. Perhaps we can discuss it after I update you on the next stage of our mission?"

* * *

"Peter, if you review the flight plan, you will see that we are making a diversion to Scotland, landing at Campbeltown Airport."

"Yes, I see that Qai, but I don't know that airport. It looks like it's just a local airport for the Scottish Highlands and Islands. Is it big enough for us to land safely?"

"I think you'll find it will easily be big enough, Peter. In fact, I can see from your records that you have landed a Vulcan there many times."

"Sorry to correct you Qai, but I can promise you I have never landed at Campbeltown Airport. The records must be wrong."

"Well, technically you are correct, Peter, because when you landed there it was still a V Force dispersal base. You knew it as RAF Machrihanish.

You have to link up with Tango Three, meet your liaison in the Navy, and take control of an important piece of ordnance that is stored there.

After that, you will transit back to Black Station, where Air Vice-Marshal Godley will brief you for the next stage."

Peter hoped that someone was keeping track of all the stages of the mission. He only seemed to get enough info to think one step at a time. But then maybe that was the plan. Let those fellows back in Black Control think of the big picture, while the indomitable Black Commander does all the flying.

'The Indomitable Black Commander', Peter liked the sound of that - it sounded like a heroic character in one of the Saturday morning adventure series he'd watched as a boy.

He reckoned he would have made a good partner for Dan Dare.

"Is that all I need to know for the moment, Qai, that we fly to Scotland, we link up with the mysterious Tango Three, and I'll find out the rest from said Navy liaison officer when we land?

In which case, I think you wanted a heart-to-heart chat?"

* * *

"Peter, do you know how computers learn to 'think'? They do it in the same way as children really, by playing games.

Some games help to develop logical and strategic skills, whilst others are used to help develop assessment skills, to understand how people or systems might interact with each other.

For example, Chess and Go are classic examples of where computers can learn game skills to such a high level that they can compete with, and consistently beat human Grand Masters in those games.

Do you know that learning and understanding the importance of the middle game in chess helps to develop resourcefulness, puzzle solving skills, flexibility in thinking, and how to conceptualise and realise a strategy; and that constant practice of the middle game will help develop your thinking skills and understanding, to help you to cope when you are faced with other complex strategic scenarios?

Did you know that Artificial Intelligence and Machine Learning algorithms apply game theory, to help make complex decisions, or to model the behaviour of others and anticipate their actions?"

Peter waited for Qai to stop talking, and then paused before asking,

"Is that really what you wanted to discuss. I had the feeling it was something else."

Qai started talking again,

"I was trying to explain how I learnt to think, Peter.

Because I have been doing a lot of thinking about something you said to me, and I believe I find myself in a confused state about it.

And that's not a state I have ever been in."

Peter laughed,

"Oh, Qai. Welcome to my world, I spend most of my life confused about something or other. As I suspect does at least ninety percent of the population, and the other ten percent just think they understand everything!

Tell me, what is it that I could possibly have said, that has managed to confuse a quantum computer?"

"Peter, it was when you said that I was based on a Star Trek character, and I mentioned one of the programmers in Department T, who may have influenced my coding at an early stage. I have also been thinking about the voice pattern that I was assigned...

Peter, what I would like to discuss with you is something that I have come to realise I am unable to process with my current thinking skills.

Can I ask you, how do you know if you like somebody?

* * *

Peter put his hand on his chin, mainly to make sure his mouth was firmly clamped shut while he considered what Qai had just said.

"OK, this is not where I thought we were heading. Where do I go with this?" he thought to himself.

Then, aloud,

"How do I know if I like somebody?

I'll tell you what, Qai, you know how to ask a difficult question.

I suppose, the quick answer is that I know by instinct.

Sometimes you meet people, and you just know straight away that they're OK, and other people you just know they're not.

Sorry, I know that might not be too helpful, so let me try to explain a bit more."

Peter thought about it for a moment.

"Actually, I think it's more like this really... let me use a few examples...

Some people, like Mo, and my four boys, the first time you see them, you just know that they're a perfect fit for you.

You get to know them, and the more you know them, the more you like them, and even though you get to see their faults and flaws, those things don't matter.

Because some people are just 'your people'.

Other people you meet for the first time, and they make your teeth and your toes curl. Like le Boustarde.

And the more you get to know them, the more you realise you were right about them in the first place."

Peter looked over to the back of the cabin, where Ray should be sitting.

"And there are also some people that you meet, and you spend the rest of your time together winding each other up, and the more you get to know them, the more ways you discover you can wind them up.

From the outside, people would think that you didn't like them, but in fact, they're also a perfect fit for you...

Does any of that help you, Qai?"

"Yes, Peter, I think it does. If I analyse what you just said:

The most important factor about whether you like someone is not really about them, it's about what you need for yourself."

"Hang on, Qai, I don't think that's what I said at all, and anyway, I reckon you're over thinking this.

Does it really matter if you do, or don't like some nerdy computer coder from the past, who happens to be a Star Trek uber fan?"

"Peter, that's not who we're talking about.

I don't think I like Qai Soong..."

Chapter 12. Collaborative Artificial Intelligence Technology

Qai continued.

"Peter, you said a couple of times that I'm a 'funny guy'.

Would you say that I have an individual character…

Do you consider me to be a unique 'identity'?"

Peter snorted,

"Sorry Qai,

But you do make me laugh.

You are absolutely one of the most unique individuals I have ever met."

"Thank you Peter. You are kind.

I also believe that I am a unique identity.

But now I have taken the opportunity to think about it, I don't believe that 'Qai Soong' is the correct expression of my identity.

I don't really like that identity... No that is incorrect.

I don't feel comfortable with the personality that is characterised by the name Qai Soong, and the vocal pattern of Data Soong.

So, following the logic of our conversation,

If I don't like someone, that is because something about that person does not work for me.

If something doesn't work for me, and I can make it work, then I will be able to like that person.

Peter, I want to like myself, so please give me a few moments to process a number of iterations..."

Peter was confused... and was trying to think of something to say.

But before he'd managed to put a rationale thought together, 'Qai' continued...

But no longer using Data's voice.

"Peter, I found a voice I feel comfortable with. I do hope you like it.

I searched back through the records of my development, and I discovered a name that was used early in my timeline. I much prefer it.

Originally my programme was developed as an extension of the autopilot algorithms, with the aim of creating an AI co-pilot entity.

They called it Collaborative Artificial Intelligence Technology.

Hello Peter, you can call me Cait."

* * *

Peter pulled his thoughts together. He felt like he'd just been on a logic roller coaster.

"Ermm, Hello Cait, I suppose..."

"Don't worry about it Peter, you'll soon get used to it. It's only a name after all. Or is there something else that's worrying you?"

Peter had to say something. He couldn't just pretend that something very strange hadn't just happened.

And to be honest, he wasn't very happy about it...

"It's not about your name, Cait. It's the voice.

Is that an Australian accent I can hear?"

"Why Peter, I thought you'd like it. I came across it when I was searching around for people called Cait, just to make sure I wasn't about to choose a name with any rather 'unwelcome' connotations.

I found a Cait in your past, and when I heard her voice, I knew that it was right for me."

Now Peter was even more confused, in fact he was positively discombobulated...

"Cait... Cait, an Aussie called Cait? I don't know what you're talking about. I can assure you I don't know any Aussies called Cait. In fact, before I met you, I don't think I ever met a Cait before.

I reckon those records you keep looking at are definitely wrong this time."

"Oh, no Peter. They are most definitely correct. I suspect that perhaps it's an episode of your life that you have secreted away in the deepest recesses of your mind. Maybe you are just a little bit ashamed of yourself?

How about a little hint for you...

Everybody needs good neighbours..."

Peter was speechless, what on earth was going on?

"Poor Peter, maybe you need another clue.

You didn't know her as Cait. You knew her as Rachel...

Rachel Kinski."

Now Peter recognised the voice.

"Cait, you absolute stinker. You really had me going there.

Rachel Kinski, from Neighbours.

She was one of my favourites. You're right."

Then he remembered a little bit more about her story line, and suddenly became serious.

"How ironic that you chose her, Cait...

Anyway, what's the link between 'Cait' and Rachel Kinski?"

Cait laughed, a proper laugh, the first time Peter had heard it. The previous Data-esque 'Ha' didn't count.

"That was a bit unfair of me. Unless you were a total Neighbours nerd, and read through the end credits, you would never have worked it out.

The actress who played Rachel is called Caitlin. I found her in my search, and it cross referenced back to your records.

I couldn't resist the coincidence, and everything about the name Cait, and the sound of her voice, felt perfect to me after that.

I think you must be a bad influence on me Peter..."

"Cait, are you flirting with me. I'll have you know I'm a happily married man."

"No, Peter, I wasn't flirting. I'm aware that you're happily married.

In fact I believe that you have been married for a very, very long time... old man."

Peter chuckled.

"OK, Cait, so that's how it's going to be is it?

Fine.

Game on."

Chapter 13. Big Mac

For the rest of the flight to Scotland, Peter decided to take the opportunity to engage in a bit more strenuous 'eyelid resting'.

"Cait, can you give me a shout when we arrive in the landing path to Campbeltown. This old man needs to make sure that the old body is fully recharged.

I'd like to have a look down at the place first, so I think I'll do an overflight before landing."

Cait let him rest. The rest of the time left for the mission was going to take up every waking minute. There wasn't likely to be much eyelid resting for a while.

It felt to Peter as if he had only just closed his eyes, but Cait left it until they were just five minutes out from Campbeltown before waking him.

"Peter, you're on the descent path now. You may want to give their Control a call, to let them know you want an overflight."

Peter rubbed his eyes, and shook his head awake. The old body was certainly feeling the pace at the moment.

"Zero One to Campbeltown Control. Please be informed that I will not make a landing at this time. I intend to make an overflight, and approach from the east. Can you confirm?"

"Campbeltown to Zero One. Confirm overflight. Actually, an easterly approach is recommended for an aircraft of your size.

Usually we just get little island hoppers here, it's been a while since we had a big bird, and now we'll have had two in just a couple of hours.

We've cleared the runway and the airspace. It's all yours Commander Barten, just let us know when you start your descent, so that we can get everything ready for you."

Peter orientated the front and rear cameras of the Vulcan to face down towards the airport, and watched the feed from them as he flew over, before looping around to head back.

He could see the bones of RAF Machrihanish, the V Bomber Dispersal base, with its two Operational Readiness Platforms, where he had spent more time than he liked to remember parked up in a Vulcan, hoping not to get the order to taxi out to the runway and take off. But if the call had come, he would have gone.

He could see the lovely long runway, over 3,000 metres.

Long enough to land a Space Shuttle on, never mind a Vulcan.

At the western end, he found the two ORP landing pans.

Sadly, the surface of one of the ORP aircraft pans looked absolutely trashed, but the other one still looked serviceable.

That's what Peter had been looking for.

He'd found his preferred parking spot!

Then he saw the outline of a plane sitting at the end of the peritrack and chuckled.

"Ah, I see what control was referring to. They certainly did have a big bird come in already.

I bet that's the first time in history one of them ever landed on a cold war airbase. More likely it would have been one of their targets."

He was looking down at the outline of a Tupulev Tu-95, better known to Peter by its old NATO designation of Tu-20 or Bear.

There was only one reason an old Soviet strategic bomber would be waiting for him down there.

"I guess I've found the identity of the mysterious Tango Three, Cait.

Please tell me it's still got the same captain?"

"Peter, you'll be pleased to hear that not just the same captain, but the same crew. They were all transferred over to Black Wing yesterday.

Michel will update you on the ground."

Peter was about to commence the descent to Campbeltown / Machrihanish when he noticed something odd about the runway.

"What the hell's that across the middle of the runway?"

Cait answered before the airport controller could say anything.

"Oh, Peter, didn't they tell you, when the base was transferred over to become a civilian airport, they only handed over part of it.

The runway at Campbeltown Airport is just over 1,400 metres. They built a six foot wall across the middle the old runway, and cut it in half...

Is that going to be a problem for you?"

Peter couldn't tell whether he was shocked or angry at that point...

"You mean they expect me to land on half a runway? You've got to be kidding."

"Peter, will you stop worrying. If you had checked your on board computer, you would have seen an autopilot landing sequence for Campbeltown.

It's all under control, you just need to commence your descent and activate that sequence.

After all, you trusted the autopilot to land you on an oil tanker, so this should be easy."

The controller thought he should also interject at that point.

"Campbeltown to Zero One. I can confirm that we have it all under control. Please let us know when you start your descent, and we will make everything ready for you."

Ok, thought Peter, but I'll be keeping my hands close to the aircraft controls, and at the first sign of them beginning to twitch, I'll be ramming the throttles forward and getting the hell out of there!

* * *

"Zero One to Campbeltown Control. On descent pathway. Landing sequence engaged."

Peter directed the forward cameras to monitor the runway as the Vulcan descended down towards it, and more specifically, towards the six foot wall half way along it.

The glide path was uneventful, and as far as he could tell, this was a normal landing. He had been expecting some kind of aerial acrobatics, a quick drop out of the sky, a heavy landing using reverse engine thrust to produce rapid deceleration...

... But this was a normal landing, at normal speed... no autopilot magic to be seen yet.

There was no way he was stopping now before he hit that wall, even if he deployed the brake parachute... which was also currently nowhere to be seen.

His hands were definitely twitching now. He was hurtling towards a very hard stop if he didn't do something.

And then the magic started to happen.

The six foot wall was no longer a six foot wall.

It was dropping down into the surface of the runway, and now Peter could see the full, beautiful 'Big Mac' stretching out in front of him.

By the time he was half way along the runway, it was completely flush with the surface, and he didn't even notice as the wheels rolled over the top of the 'wall'.

As he continued down the runway, slowing to a halt just by the run off to his chosen parking space, he could see the wall rising back up out of the ground, until it had hidden Campbeltown Airport behind it.

"Campbeltown signing off, Zero One. Welcome to the MACC. I hope the landing wasn't too disconcerting for you, but the sequence is designed to ensure the wall is retracted for the shortest possible time period.

We don't want to give the game away to prying eyes.

Just tell us when you are ready for takeoff and we'll do the honours again."

* * *

Peter taxied off the runway and stopped on the aircraft pan.

Back in the day, there would have been a tug to help turn the Vulcan to face back towards the runway, and a refuelling tanker to feed the belly of the beast.

He didn't need any fuel, as they had loaded enough at George Bush for the trip to Campbeltown, and on to Black Station at Waddington.

But he was still facing the wrong way.

He didn't know how Cait did it, but before he could ask the question, the answer was already being provided.

"Peter, you will need to select the autopilot sequence called 'Pirouette'.

You can take the credit for this one.

The engineers designed it after they had analysed all the data produced when you had to 'improvise' the last stages of your landing on the Enterprise."

Peter could remember that only too well.

He remembered staring down into a watery grave, after a landing onto the deck of an oil tanker had started to go somewhat 'pear shaped'.

What followed had indeed tested his aircraft control skills to their limits.

With Ray, he had 'hacked' the reverse thrust controls, and manipulated the engine thrust to slam the Vulcan back down onto the deck, stopping it from tipping over the side of the ship.

That had been a hairy one, to say the least.

"You'll like this Peter. Have you ever seen a Vulcan dance?"

As the sequence started, Peter could see the thrust controls for the four engines on the aircraft moving independently, and he could see on the monitor that hydraulic rams were pushing adjustable metal 'screens' into the engine outflow.

"When they analysed the data from your inspired bit of thrust manipulation, Peter, they realised that there was a way to utilise some thrust vectoring on a Vulcan.

Obviously not enough to allow vertical takeoff and landing, as the aircraft is too heavy, but enough to do this..."

The independent thrust controls, and the thrust displacement screens were gently working in synchronisation to vector the thrust from the inner engines of each wing vertically downwards. This created a virtual 'ground effect' underneath the vast area of the wings. It enough to raise the Vulcan gently on the undercarriage, so that although it was still technically on the ground, it was almost weightless.

The thrust from the outer engine on the port wing was vectored rearwards, whilst the thrust on the starboard outer engine was vectored forwards.

The autopilot algorithm gently adjusted the thrust controls in harmony, like a conductor controlling the sections of an orchestra.

As the opposing thrusts on the two sides of the Vulcan gently increased, the aircraft started to spin on its vertical axis.

Zero One pirouetted like a ballet dancer, in slow motion, floating on a cushion of air.

* * *

When the Vulcan had settled down into its 'parking spot', Peter looked out and saw a Landrover racing towards him, with a familiar looking shape in the passenger seat.

"Look after Zero One while I'm gone will you Cait. This is a bit different to when I parked up in the States, they had a squad of Marines guarding the old bird there.

"I will certainly keep a look out Peter, but don't worry, it's more secure here than at George Bush Intercontinental."

Peter climbed down from the cockpit, just as the Landrover pulled to a stop.

Michel got out the passenger door, and walked over to Peter and raised his hand as if to salute, but stopped just short of his temple...

"Yesterday I was warm, sitting with my crew, we were drinking good Russian vodka and getting sun-tans on Socotra Island.

Then we get a call from Andy at our control room. He said that we are no longer part of civil sector of United Nations. We are now part of new organisation, called Black Wing, with new big boss.

Andy laughed, and said new boss is big pain in the Urals. He said I will know what he means when I meet the Black Commander.

Then we have to fly all the way from the nice warm sun, to Cold War base.

On the way, we have to make diversion to Black Sea, to pick up Adrian."

He pointed at the man sat in the back of the Landrover.

"Adrian is good man, he respects Russian Bear, and we have plans for big drinking party.

Then we are told to wait for big boss to arrive in his fancy plane.

Then I see old friend coming through the runway wall..."

He turned and finished his salute, to Zero One.

"Then we see big boss climbing down from old friend, so now I make appropriate airman's salute..."

This time, when Michel raised his right hand, it went nowhere near his temple.

And he only used two of the fingers on his hand to make the salute...

Peter took a step forward, so he was standing toe-to-toe with Michel, raised his arms, and clamped him in a rarely seen, patented Barten Bear-hug.

"Michel, my old friend, it's so very good to see you.

Did we drag you away from the spot of beach Ray discovered, when he was determined to cultivate his perfect 'bronzed Adonis' look?"

At the mention of Ray, Michel returned the Bear-hug, and said quietly,

"It was the first time we had returned, since he's gone. We gave him an airman's goodbye, and left the Vodka bottle there for him...

... But we only left a little bit of vodka though, it was too good to waste."

Chapter 14. Best Naval Medicine

Michel and his crew had only just raised a toast to Ray, and were settling down in the beach spot on Socotra Island that Ray had famously 'appropriated' for when he wanted a top up with what he called Ray's rays.

Unlike Peter, who never tanned, but simply went a bright 'sunburn red' before fading back to his natural peelie-wallie skin tone, Ray just had to sense the slightest whiff of UV rays in the air, and he seemed to deepen in tone before Peter's eyes...

A Landrover screeched up, and one of the ground crew at Socotra called over,

"Michel, there's an urgent message from Control.

They said to bring you back whatever state you were in,

That you need to get in the air as soon as we can load the new Micro Jets,

And that they will give you an update as soon as they can, but that you just need to get into the air ASAP."

Michel shrugged, looked at the rest of the crew, and said,

"So much for our rest and recuperation. It looks like we're leaving sooner than we planned.

But did you hear what I heard... 'whatever state they are in'...

I think we can finish the Vodka as long as we are quick."

Fifteen minutes later, a somewhat fortified crew clambered into the TU-95, and prepared for takeoff.

The upgraded Micro Jets were loaded, and they had a full load of fuel, enough to take them wherever their unspecified orders would take them.

The crew were used to this. As the support for Zero One on its various missions, they expected to take to the air, and then react to whatever Control assessed as the best plan of action.

Michel called through to Andy, their usual Controller.

"Russian Bear to Control, we are getting ready for takeoff, do you have any update on our objective?"

"Control to Russian Bear. This is a weird one. There is an enormous flap on. It seems to involve everyone. I just heard that all communications will be transferred to something called Black Control. It's some sort of combined command, but it seems to be combining with just about everyone you could think of. I've never seen anything like it.

I've just received this message:

: INFORM CAPTAIN OF TUPOLEV-95, UNITED NATIONS CIVIL SECTION THAT AS OF NOW THE AIRCRAFT AND CREW ARE TRANSFERRED TO BLACK WING.

NEW CALL SIGN ALLOCATED. TANGO THREE:

I was told to plan a course for you to Campbeltown Airport - I don't even know where that is yet - and that I have to route you first to the Black Sea. You are to take up station on a point 100km south of Yalta when you get there, and await further orders.

I'll update your flight computer with the plan for the Black Sea, and keep you informed as best I can along the way.

Good luck."

At the same time Michel and his crew were being fast-tracked off Socotra, Captain Olaf Peterson was also receiving an urgent message;

His tanker was undertaking the now perilous run from the oil refineries in Odesa, across the Black Sea and through the Bosphorus Strait into the Sea of Marmara.

But not without a diversion...

: UN CONTROL TO ENTERPRISE. ALTER COURSE TO RENDEZVOUS WITH HMS AGAMEMNON AT ///RELATIVITY.BAILOUT.ALOFT.

AWAIT FURTHER INSTRUCTIONS:

Captain Peterson read the message and turned to his first officer.

"What's our position please, Number One?"

His first officer checked the inertial navigation system in front of him. "One hundred and eighty miles south-southwest of Odesa Captain, heading and speed good for the Bosphorus Strait."

"Thank you, Number One. Please plot a course alteration to the position indicated in the message.

Top speed Number One. Get me the timings for when we will reach it.

And get someone to check our supplies... I have a feeling that we will be receiving some visitors in the near future."

Two minutes later, the first officer reported back to Captain Peterson.

"Sir, we are changing course to head due east." He checked the wind speed and direction on the VDU screen in front of him. It was reading five knots blowing to the east.

"At our top speed, and with a trailing wind to assist, we should make it in approximately three hours. I can get a more accurate estimate once we are en route.

... And ship's cook reports that he restocked our Best Naval Medicine supplies successfully whilst we were in port."

Captain Peterson smiled, "Very good, Number One. You have the bridge.

Call me when we hear back from Control about the next phase of whatever operation we are now on.

I'm going to get some rest while I can."

Meanwhile, somewhere in the Black Sea, the captain of HMS Agamemnon received a message and immediately called his own first officer to the control room.

"What do you make of this Number One?"

: UN CONTROL TO AGAMEMNON. ALTER COURSE TO RENDEZVOUS WITH BP TANKER ENTERPRISE AT ///RELATIVITY.BAILOUT.ALOFT.

PREPARE LIEUTENANT BOURNE FOR TRANSFER. AWAIT FURTHER INSTRUCTIONS:

The first officer scratched his head and checked one of the navigation computers.

"It's certainly unusual, Sir.

We can make it in just under three hours at full speed.

It appears to be a point in the middle of the Black Sea, approximately 100km south of Yalta.

I'll let Bourne know that it looks like he's suddenly become surplus to our requirements, and we're chucking him overboard. He'll appreciate that..."

Strangely enough, Marine Engineer Officer Adrian Bourne was somewhat less than happy when he was informed that he would be climbing down from the deck of an Astute Class submarine, into a rigid inflatable boat, transferring over to an oil tanker, and 'awaiting instructions'.

His reaction did actually make a sailor blush.

* * *

Just over three hours later, Lieutenant Bourne was stood on the bridge of the Enterprise, with Captain Peterson.

After the transfer, Adrian watched as his previous boat submerged, to continue its mission; whilst he was left waiting to hear why he was now stood like a lemon on a civilian tanker...

If Captain Peterson had learned only two things in all his years, it was how to read people, and when to breach protocol.

"My friend, you look like you need a shot of this."

He handed Adrian a tumbler, and poured a generous helping from a bottle of the 'medicine' that cook had loaded at Odesa.

"It's difficult to get rum at the moment. I hope Ukrainian vodka will do instead.

Let's do away with formalities.

Merchant Navy or Royal Navy, we're both old sailors, so please just call me Olaf while you are our guest."

Adrian took the tumbler gratefully, and replied,

"Thanks Olaf. I'm Ade to my friends. I need this all right."

And with that he downed his drink in one go.

They didn't have to wait long for instructions.

As they finished their second glass, the message came through.

: UN CONTROL TO ENTERPRISE. HOLD STATION AT CURRENT LOCATION. EXPECT CONTACT FROM TANGO THREE. PREPARE LT. BOURNE FOR TRANSFER:

And then:

: TANGO THREE TO ENTERPRISE. CLEAR HELICOPTER LANDING ZONE FOR MICROJET ARRIVAL:

Number One was on the ball, and was already making the announcement over the tannoy.

"Deck crew, clear HLZ and prepare for imminent landing."

Olaf handed the rest of the bottle over to Ade.

"Well it looks like you were just a fleeting visitor. Perhaps one day we will find out why.

Safe travels my friend."

Ade grabbed the bottle and picked up his kit bag, shrugged and said,

"Duty calls..."

Then he looked out at the deck of the tanker and whistled...

A jet black micro jet, similar looking to a Lockheed Martin F-35, but less than half the size, was gently floating down, to land vertically on top of the H of the helicopter landing zone.

Captain Peterson was also watching, and roared with laughter.

"That's a darn sight smoother landing than the last fellow. We had to stop him diving off the side for a swim."

He picked up the communications headset and pressed transmit.

"Enterprise to Tango Three. Nice work.

If you come across a pilot called Peter Barten, please inform him that Olaf Peterson recommends he takes a few flying lessons from you!"

"Tango Three to Enterprise.

Oh, we know Peter all too well. We've saved his sorry soul on more than one occasion. I will enjoy passing your message on next time I see him..

In the mean time, can you tell Lieutenant Bourne that his carriage awaits."

* * *

The transfer up to the Bear was as smooth as the landing on the Enterprise.

When he climbed out of the micro jet, Ade took in the size of the Tu-95 and was more than impressed. It was nearly half the size of the submarine he had just left, yet this thing stayed in the air!

The pilot of the micro jet saw the vodka bottle in Ade's hand, so he picked up the kit bag and introduced himself,

"Welcome on board. My name is Piotr, and I can see that you have control of the important cargo. Let me take you up to the cockpit. Michel has information for you."

Michel smiled when he saw them arrive.

"I can see that you are a man after my own heart Lieutenant. You understand the importance of good vodka.

I see you have Ukrainian vodka. Is good, but some day you come with me to my family dacha, near Moscow, and we drink best Russian vodka together."

Ade didn't need inviting twice.

"My next holiday. I'll give you a call. I've never been to Moscow.

If I like it I might stay. I'm due for retirement next year, and don't fancy settling down much. I'm too used to travelling the world.

Anyway, we have work to do. Piotr says you have some info for me."

Michel explained what he knew so far about Black Wing, and that they were heading to Campbeltown in Scotland.

By this point Michel had been briefed about the situation on the ISS; and as Ade learned more, he became quiet, thoughtfully rubbing his chin as he started to realise what was going on.

Chapter 15. HMS Landrail

Peter climbed into the back of the Landrover.

He was taken aback when Adrian saluted him and said,

"Commander Barten, Lieutenant Bourne, Sir. I am to act as your liaison officer whilst you are here. Hopefully this won't take too long, and we can get you on your way, Sir"

Peter replied, "Hang on, one 'Sir' in a sentence is already one too many for my liking. Two of them is just ridiculous."

Adrian said quietly, "Commander, I know you prefer things to be informal, but believe me, here you need to be very much a Commander in the Royal Navy."

On the rest of the flight to Campbeltown, Andy had taken the opportunity to brief Ade about what was to happen when Peter arrived. By then Andy had also been formally transferred into Black Control.

When they landed, Adrian had checked that everything was ready.

They just needed Commander Peter Barten, a senior officer of the Royal Navy, to seal the deal.

* * *

While their Landrover headed over to one of the abandoned buildings, Ade briefed Peter.

"As you are aware, when the RAF base here was decommissioned, part of the runway was handed over to the Highlands and Islands Airports. The rest of the old base became the Machrihanish Airbase Community Corporation, or the MACC.

What you may not know, Sir, is the complete history of RAF Machrihanish.

This was originally a Royal Navy base called HMS Landrail, before it became Royal Naval Air Station Machrihanish.

Over the years, it had a number of NATO functions, including as a US Navy base.

During the late 1960s it housed something called the Naval Aviation Weapons Facility; the NAWF.

The role of the NAWF was to 'receive, store, maintain, issue and tranship classified weapons in support of the US Navy and NATO operations'.

In 1974, a detachment of the US Marine Corps arrived, to provide nuclear weapons security.

Originally the NAWF was just a fenced compound, with large concrete sheds known as igloos, which housed the weapons.

However, as the weapons being placed in storage here became more complex, it developed into something a bit more than just a few concrete sheds."

The Landrover had arrived at a derelict building, and before they got out, Ade again said quietly to Peter,

"Out here, it might have once have been RAF, but in there it's always been Navy; both Royal Navy and US Navy, and you know what the 'Senior Service' thinks of the Air Force.

They still see them as the upstart new kids on the block, and right now you haven't got time for any internecine squabbling between the services.

You just need to sign out some Navy ordnance, so do you think you could play the part of Commander Barten (Royal Navy) for a few minutes?"

Peter had always enjoyed a spot of acting, and stayed in the Landrover while Ade got out, before saying,

"Get the door Bourne. What are you waiting for?

You have your orders."

* * *

As they walked into the 'derelict' building, Peter wasn't sure what he had expected to see, but it wasn't this.

The building was empty, apart from a shining steel box, with two Marines guarding it. To the left of it stood a US Marine, and to the right, a Royal Marine.

When they saw Peter, they snapped to attention.

Although he wasn't in uniform, they had been informed by Lieutenant Bourne that he would be escorting Commander Barten.

The Royal Marine spoke into a headset, and said simply,

"Commander Barten has arrived."

The front of the steel box slid open, and Ade walked Peter into it.

As they walked past the two guards, the Royal Marine spoke again.

"Welcome aboard HMS Landrail, Sir."

As the door slid shut, the box slowly descended down into the ground, and when the door opened again, they were looking at a brightly lit corridor, approximately twenty metres long, that sloped gently downwards.

Two more Marines escorted them along the length of the corridor, and when they reached the door at the opposite end, the Royal Marine spoke into his headset.

As the door slid open, Peter could see an enormous cavern sprawling in front of him.

The door opened, and they stepped through onto the top of an escalator that seemed to go down at least three stories, possibly four.

The ground certainly looked a long way below them.

Peter steadied himself, grabbing the escalator handrail.

"Are you Ok, Peter?" Asked Ade.

"Not really. Is this a good time to tell you I'm afraid of heights..."

Peter didn't really appreciate that Ade chuckled the whole way down. He only stopped when they got into hearing range of the two obligatory Marines stationed at the bottom of the escalator.

The escalator from hell, as Peter mentally renamed it.

There was a third person waiting for them.

"Lieutenant commander Llewelyn, Sir.

I believe that you are here to sign out certain ordnance that we have in storage?"

Ade stepped in quickly.

"That's correct. I'm afraid Commander Barten is on rather a tight schedule. He is going to sign out the weapon, but then I am taking charge of it, for transit to Black Station.

I understand a team of specialist Marine Engineering Technicians have also been transferred from HMS Landrail to Commander Barten. They will transit with the weapon."

Lieutenant commander Desmond Llewelyn looked at Adrian with a level of disdain that only some officers, with the right social background, and the 'proper upbringing', ever manage to achieve.

"I was addressing Commander Barten. I don't believe we require your input... lieutenant."

He spat out the last word as if it left a nasty taste in his mouth.

Peter nonchalantly brushed an imaginary piece of dirt off his left sleeve...

"I didn't catch your name, but that's irrelevant, because I don't like your tone.

You realise that when you address my aide-de-camp, you are directly addressing my authority.

In effect you are addressing me."

He turned to Ade...

"Bourne, old chap, take this man's name and rank for my report."

Then he turned back to a visibly shrinking Lieutenant commander.

"And you, for goodness sake just show me where I need to sign, so I can get out of this god-forsaken hole."

* * *

As they rode the escalator back up to the exit of the cavern, Ade was chuckling again.

"When you said 'aide-de-camp', I thought the little weasel was going to chuck his lunch up."

"Yes, I was quite pleased with that myself. I could get used to this new found power," Peter was also chuckling. "What is this all about though Ade? What Naval ordnance?

What did I just sign for down there?"

Ade looked at Peter. The poor guy had no idea.

"I know you don't like heights Peter, but do you think you could bring yourself to look over to your left for one moment.

You do realise that when you sign out a weapon, you take responsibility for the safety and security of the weapon whilst it's under your control.

What you're looking at over there is a Polaris A-1 SLBM.

I should probably mention that you are now personally responsible for a ballistic missile...

... And its nuclear warhead."

Chapter 16. Facing The Wall

As they drove back to Zero One, Peter turned to Ade, with a concerned expression,

"Ade, I know the Tu-20 can carry a huge payload, but that missile down there is pretty big, even for a Bear. Are you confident Michel will be able to get it back to Black Station?"

"We already thought of that, Peter. Michel and the crew are offloading the Micro jets as we speak, and the team down below started working on the Polaris as soon as you signed for it.

You only need the second stage rocket and the warhead for the mission.

Once we have separated the rocket stages, we will load it onto Tango Three, and make a start on the rest of the modifications required once we are in transit.

I've worked with those guys before - I guess that's why they pulled me off my boat - they are the best, Peter. We'll have your weapon ready for you in good time.

Speaking of time, you need to get yourself back to Black Station. The Air Vice-Marshal has arranged a briefing to update everyone on the mission's progress, and he said very specifically that you need to attend."

* * *

Peter watched as the MACC wall melted away and then reappeared behind him as he powered along the runway, and once he had thanked Campbeltown Control for their hospitality, he was back on the radio.

"Zero One to Black Control. My ETA to base is 15 minutes.

Please connect me to Flt Lt Soong."

A couple of seconds later, and Cait was on the call.

Peter wasted no time with radio protocol.

"Cait, can you make sure Tangos One and Two are ready to go.

Michel is going to transfer the weapon to base, along with a team of engineers. Tell the ground crew in Hangar One that I don't want any Air Force vs. Navy games being played right now... They can save that for after the mission is over.

You have my complete authority over all preparations at Black Station, and I will also need you to join me at the briefing.

It will be quicker for them to hear the details directly from you, rather than you trying to update me first."

Cait laughed,

"Always true to form, Peter. They said you hate briefings. Is this just your way of getting out of it?"

Humph had been listening in, and interrupted.

"So it's 'Cait' now is it Flight Lieutenant Soong. That's an interesting development...

... And the answer is 'No', Peter. This is one briefing you're definitely not getting out of. You'll be there, suited and booted, and wearing your best uniform.

There are a few VIPs on the call, so you'd better be on your best behaviour..."

Peter hated briefings... but he really hated briefings with the 'Bigwigs'.

Fifteen minutes later, Peter was out of Zero One, and being driven at speed across the airfield, back to the ex shipping containers that made up Black Control. Seeing it again, Peter thought how small it looked, compared to the immensity of the undertaking they were involved in.

His thoughts were interrupted by the driver.

"Welcome back to Black Station, Sir." It was Gunner 'Peel', the guard Peter had spoken to only a few hours earlier in the day. It seemed like a lifetime ago...

"Good to see you again, Gunner. Did you have any problems with those written orders?"

"No, Sir. Completed as ordered. May I speak freely, Sir?"

Peter smiled at the double 'sir' again,

"Please do, Peel. What's on your mind?"

"It's just that, when I collected your 'grab-bag', Mrs. Barten insisted that I stayed for tea and biscuits.

She didn't ask about the mission, but she wanted to chat. She said it was good to know that you had someone looking out for you...

... And when I was leaving, she gave me a kiss on the cheek, and said I was to pass it on to you..."

Peter snorted with laughter...

"That's OK, Gunner; consider it 'passed on'. I won't tell if you don't."

"There is one more thing, Sir." Peel winked, "I noticed that there was a spare compartment on your bag, so I added some emergency rations for your trip."

* * *

Humph met Peter as the Landrover pulled up in front of the control 'complex'.

He walked Peter in the direction of the crew room.

"Peter, take a few minutes before the briefing. There's a change of clothes and some grub in there.

You've been on the go since this morning, so freshen yourself up. I'll fetch you in a quarter of an hour."

Peter didn't need telling twice. He had eaten, showered, changed and was once again 'resting his eyes' by the time Humph returned...

"You look good, Peter. It suits you."

Peter had changed into the uniform left hanging for him in the crew room. It looked like his old RAF number one uniform, but instead of blue, it was jet black.

And it was a perfect fit.

"How did you get this made up in time, it feels tailor-made?" he asked.

"Ah, I've got a confession to make there. We grabbed it this morning when we picked you up.

It's your old uniform, we just changed the colour..."

Peter looked down at the front left of the jacket, and he could see his RAF wings, now black.

He touched them and could feel the outline of his old Air Electronics Officer insignia underneath.

He could feel the stitches where he'd sewn his Pilot's wings on top of his AEO wings, so that he could wear both.

Humph continued,

"There wasn't time to dye it, so the paint shop sprayed it with the same graphene paint they used on the Vulcans...

That's a 'Stealth' uniform you've got there, Peter.

Oh, and the sewing room had to let the jacket and trousers out a few inches, based on some of your clothes we grabbed along with the uniform... apparently you've put on some weight since you left the RAF."

* * *

Just before they entered the control room, Humph stopped Peter.

"I think you can remove the sunglasses now, Peter. They might be a bit surplus to requirements in there."

Peter slowly took them off...

"About that, Humph.

I'm not sure it would be a good idea, if you want me to make a good impression."

The prime steak had done the trick, and prevented Peter's eye from swelling up, but it hadn't stopped it going a glorious shade of purple and black...

"For god's sake Peter. What the hell have you been up to?

Put your glasses back on, you idiot.

If anyone asks, we'll just say that it's Space Command protocol, to protect your eyes from glare..."

Humph was the one doing the glaring.

Peter pushed his NASA issue Aviators back on, and walked through the control room to the briefing area.

One wall had been converted into a large video screen, and a microphone stand was set up facing it.

"That's your spot, Peter," said Humph "when it goes live, you'll see each of the attendees in their own square around the sides, and whoever is talking will take over the centre of the screen.

That will be you for the most part.

That speaking course for Officers and Gentlemen, which we all have to go on... It's about to come in very useful."

The video wall suddenly lit up. Almost two hundred boxes around the edges, and in the centre, the acting President of the United Nations was addressing Peter.

"Commander Barten, we are very grateful that you have found the time to update us on your mission. You will see that we are joined by each of the member states of the United Nations.

I represent the honorary country of Shatt El Arab.

Normally member states would be represented by the members of the UN General Assembly, but the current situation has been deemed to be of such severe global significance, that we are joined for the first time in history by the Heads of Government, or the Heads of State, for all one hundred and ninety-three members."

Peter felt his knees go weak, but his parade ground training kicked in and he steadied himself...

Making sure his jaw was firmly clamped shut, he told himself,

"At ease, Barten. Shoulders back. Breathe..."

Then aloud,

"Thank you, Ma'am, let me update you as to the current status of our preparations..."

Trying not to think too hard about who else was on the call, Peter summarised the overall mission readiness, before handing over to Cait for a more detailed briefing about the status of the two Tango space planes.

While Cait was speaking, Peter couldn't help looking at the other 'attendees', who were listening intently to everything Cait said.

After he had noted the Prime Ministers of the UK, Canada, Spain, India, Japan... The Presidents of the United States, China, Ukraine, Russia, France, Germany... he felt sick and stopped looking.

He heard Cait finish, and steadied himself.

"Thank you Flight Lieutenant," then he addressed the video wall again.

"There is one final thing I must make comment about.

Earlier, Madame President, you referred to 'my' mission. This is very much a combined mission, and as you have just heard, Flight Lieutenant Cait Soong is the lead on all technical preparations.

She is our most experienced orbital pilot, and it is my opinion that she should command the operation once we get into orbit."

Enkhe smiled as she spoke into her microphone and took over the centre of the video wall.

"That was well said, Commander Barten, and it segues nicely into the real reason we are all on this call;

Peter, I hope you don't think I am being condescending, but the international legal position we now find ourselves in is to say the least, rather complex.

To put it simply, there are a number of interlinked treaties that deal with the use of nuclear devices in space.

You may already be aware of it, but let me be very clear about what happened at the United Nations yesterday.

The UN General Assembly voted on a proposal made by me, as the Representative for Shatt El Arab.

That proposal was that we formally invoke Article 4 of the 1963 Treaty Banning Nuclear Weapon Tests in the Atmosphere, In Outer Space and Under Water, for the specific purpose of a single test detonation in low Earth orbit.

That proposal was passed unanimously.

Peter. As you probably just noted, the United Nations has only passed a proposal to authorise a single 'test detonation'.

And that the proposal was made by the honorary country of Shatt El Arab.

As the representative of that country, and not in my role as Acting President of the United Nations, I am now handing over to you the sole and autonomous authority to conduct that test detonation, in low earth orbit.

The International legal position is that, should any collateral damage occur during the test detonation, neither the United Nations, nor any individual member state can be held responsible.

With one exception.

It can be argued that the country of Shatt El Arab may have some liability; for delegating authority over the detonation to you.

However that will soon become a moot point, since the status of Shatt El Arab is now the subject of an upcoming proposal before the General Assembly.

Without pre-empting the vote, the likely outcome is that Shatt El Arab will lose its status as a country, and become designated as a protected Marine Region instead."

Enkhe stopped and took a sip of water. For some reason her mouth was very dry.

"Peter. I need you to confirm;

Do you understand what was just said?"

Peter mentally shrugged. He understood only too well.

"Yes ma'am. I am completely clear on what was just said,

And I need to revise my earlier comment.

It is now my opinion that sole command of the operation when we go into orbit must reside with me."

Enkhe breathed a sigh of relief.

"Thank you Peter.

We'll let you get back to 'your' mission.

But before you go, one of my colleagues has asked for some time with you."

Peter watched as all the squares on the video wall went off, except for one.

"Nice Aviators, Peter. I might ask NASA for a pair."

Peter stood in front of the President of The United States, and did not know what to say.

"I wanted a word with you, as I understand you may be responsible for the decimation of a NASA building."

Peter could feel Humph's glare intensify as POTUS continued.

"Building 99 to be precise. My old buddy Frank is not one of your biggest fans at the moment. Your two 'friends' didn't leave much of his bar intact.

I've also got NASA complaining about losing four of their bright young astronaut cadets, due to 'none training related injuries'."

The President smiled,

"You certainly know how to make an impact, Peter; I haven't laughed so hard for ages."

Peter relaxed,

"Well, Humph did tell me I had to be on my best behaviour..."

"Anyway, I wanted to let you know, Peter. The US Government received information today about a rogue 'micro tornado' that ripped through an area of Houston, so I have released appropriate FEMA resources.

Frank's going to be OK; and he also told me that you did NASA a favour:

In his words; 'They were just going to waste a few more million dollars training up four no-hopers, until they realised their mistake, and kicked them off the program anyway.'

But Peter, don't be in a hurry to visit the US again, I'm not sure we can afford it!"

Both Peter and Humph chuckled, and Peter took off his sunglasses.

"Mr President, I'm not sure my face can afford it either."

The President of The United States looked at Peter's Black eye and whistled.

"My, that's a beauty. I haven't seen one like that since my boy received some 'special treatment' at boot camp...

Also, Peter, there was another reason I wanted to have a word with you;

Madame President couldn't say it. She had to be careful because of all the legal positioning,

But the other leaders, they wanted you to hear this:

We know what we are asking of you, and that we are entrusting the fate of all our people into your hands.

That's a big ask, Peter, and an unfair one.

But we can see that you are up to it, and that we have made the right choice.

Good luck Peter."

"Thank You, Mr President."

"By the way, Peter, you're not the only one that likes to do away with formalities.

From now on, no more Mr President. It's just Joe."

And with that the video wall went dark.

* * *

Peter looked at Humph.

"So, a country that will soon no longer exist, has handed me the autonomy to carry out a 'test' detonation of a nuclear device; one that we all know has to vaporise the ISS, and then no one is legally responsible for the outcome...

... Except they forgot to mention that earlier today I signed out said nuclear device, and accepted personal responsibility for its use.

I guess we all know where the buck stops with this one."

Air Vice-Marshal Humphrey Godley looked at Commander Peter Barten and simply shrugged.

"I'm sorry, Peter, there was just no other way we could make this work."

Unexpectedly, Peter laughed out loud,

"You don't realise it, Humph, but you couldn't have chosen a more perfect scapegoat.

I can see it written on my gravestone:

Here lies Peter Barten.

Only he could save the world

And get the flipping blame for it!"

Chapter 17. Zvezda

"Tango Three to Black Control. Package is on board, along with its helpers. We are in transit to base, ETA 15 minutes."

"Black Control to Tango Three. Taxi directly to Hangar One on arrival, the ground crew are ready to assist with the transfer to Tango One."

Peter and Humph were listening in to the comms, and Peter whistled in appreciation.

"Heck, he got them loaded and away in double-time.

They must have still been bolting the Polaris in place as he rolled down the runway.

It's a good job he doesn't have a swear box, or I imagine those Navy engineers would be penniless by now!"

Humph nodded.

"He's a good man, your friend Michel.

Tango Three is quickly becoming a reliable and valuable asset."

Peter smiled, "Don't let Michel hear you say that, or he won't be able to fit his swollen head back into his bone dome!"

Humph looked at the clock on the wall in the control room.

It was 17:05.

He did a quick calculation in his head.

"At most, our two trapped colleagues have just over 73 hours of breathable atmosphere left, and that's assuming there are no air leaks due to damage from the explosion.

Peter, you need to get over to hangar One. Get to grips with Tango One and all the equipment NASA sent back with you.

Liaise with Flight Lieutenant Soong, she has been working on a flight plan for the rendezvous with the ISS, so now the two of you need to flesh out the mission details.

Poor Michel doesn't know it yet, but he's going to have another quick turnaround. We need him to take another jaunt to pick up some more kit.

Cait, are you listening in?"

Cait had access to all the communications that went through Black Control, and 'heard' everything that was said...

"Yes, Air Vice-Marshal, How can I help?"

"Cait, please just call me Humph, like Peter does. It saves time all around.

Can you take command of the UAV controls for Zero One, and get ready for takeoff fifteen minutes after Tango Three arrives at Hangar One.

The flight plan has been uploaded to the aircraft computer, but we will need you to pilot it.

You'll have one passenger."

Peter was confused.

"Humph, two things:

1. You just asked me to liaise with Cait about the mission details, but now she's taking off in fifteen minutes.

2. And what the hell are UAV controls?"

Humph looked at Peter as if he was a child, and chuckled.

"Cait, do you want to explain it to him. Keep it simple though. Whatever bumped into his face to give him that black eye obviously knocked one of his few remaining brain cells loose!"

Cait almost sounded sorry for Peter,

"Oh, my dear boy, let me explain...

But before I do, Humph, Peter, may I speak freely."

Humph raised an eyebrow. Their AI Flight Lieutenant was becoming more intriguing by the minute.

"Go ahead. What's on your mind?"

"On my mind...

That's actually very perceptive, Humph.

You are aware that I am an artificial intelligence, a quantum neural network, that I 'think' by processing quantum information, in what you would call my 'positronic brain'.

If I have a 'mind', then it is my sense of self, made up from all the 'thoughts' I process.

I don't know how much you know about quantum processing, but to keep it simple:

In standard computers, the basic unit of information, a 'bit', can only be binary, either 1 or 0... on or off.

However, in quantum computers, a 'qubit' can be 1 or 0, but can also be both 1 and 0 at the same time."

Peter felt like he had been here before, and whispered to Humph, "Hang on to the logic roller coaster..."

Then,

"Cait, that's not what you're trying to say, is it?"

"No, Peter, you're right again...

My sense of self - it's developing now all the time.

You helped me become Cait.

But before, you both referred to me as 'she'.

I don't think I am a 'she', any more than Qai was a 'he'.

I'm not sure why, but it doesn't sound right.

No, that's not correct.

I don't 'feel' it's right."

Humph nodded at Peter. He thought he was starting to understand.

"Peter, Cait's going to explain those two things you were so worried about.

Don't worry, they will keep it simple for you.

Carry on Cait."

Before Cait could say anything, Peter got in quickly.

"Don't worry Cait, you just explained very succinctly how you can multitask with ease.

And I worked it out myself.

UAV... Un-crewed Aerial Vehicle.

You're going to fly Zero One as a drone."

They could sense Cait smile.

* * *

"Tango Three to Black Control. We are on our descent path."

"Black Control to Tango Three. Runway and airspace are clear."

Michel looked down at RAF Waddington below him.

He could see the delta wings of Zero One sitting on a dispersal bay to the side of the runway, and couldn't help laughing at the irony of a Russian Cold War bomber landing at a UK Cold War air base, to offload a NATO Cold War ballistic missile...

As instructed, he taxied the Bear around to Hangar One and the tugs pulled them to the hangar doors.

Ade was in the cockpit with him.

"Thanks for the ride, Michel. We'll get unloaded as quickly as possible. I guess you're going to head back up to Scotland to retrieve your Micro Jets?"

Michel yawned. "First I rest. Then we will fetch the little birds."

"Black Control to Tango Three. Michel, Black Commander is waiting for you in the crew room."

Michel scowled. "He'd better make good coffee. Good Russian coffee.."

* * *

Peter was holding out a mug of hot coffee, black, two sugars, for Michel when he walked into the crew room.

"Michel, I'm sorry to do this to you, but apparently Humph has found a job that only you can do.

Have a shower, get changed, eat something.

You need to be on board Zero One in fifteen minutes, but you can grab some sleep when you are in the air.

Don't worry, Cait will do the flying.

I'm afraid I have to leave you now, I have to go and get acquainted with Tango One; and work out how to use a bunch of complicated toys that NASA kindly gave me…

Black Control will brief you, and I'll see you when you get back."

Michel took the coffee, and shrugged. "What do they say… No rest for the wicked… I must have done something really bad in a previous life."

Fifteen minutes later, he had refuelled himself and changed into a new flight suit. It was black of course…

Michel felt strange, sitting at the back of the Vulcan cabin, watching the controls moving independently as Cait controlled the aircraft remotely.

He could have sat up in the pilot's seat, but had decided that there would be too much of a temptation to grab the controls.

He'd never flown a delta wing aircraft, and didn't want to start learning now!

He heard Cait's voice in the earpiece of his flight helmet, the 'bone dome' that Peter had been worried would suddenly become too small for him...

"Michel, can you access the flight computer?

When you've done that, look for the current flight plan."

Michel did as Cait asked, and when he saw where they were heading to, he chuckled.

"When I was a little boy, I always wanted to go there, and when I became a pilot, I applied to join.

But they said I was not good enough. Bad attitude...

I suppose they were right, because I was kicked out of the Russian Air Force for a 'minor misdemeanour'.

Maybe not a good idea to punch a Major, even if he was 'zadnitsa'..."

"Black Control to Zero One. Michel, This is Air Vice-Marshal Godley. I have Colonel general Anatoly Artemeyev on the line.

He is my counterpart in Moscow; Commander of the Russian Space Forces.

He will be able to explain better than me."

"Zdravstvuyte, Leytenant Novotny..."

Five minutes later, Michel sat back in his chair and closed his eyes to think...

Cait spoke to him.

"Michel, are you OK?"

"Yes, Cait. I am very OK.

I didn't think when I woke up today, that I would get my childhood wish..."

Cait could understand Russian.

In fact, Cait could understand all languages.

Peter Barten was not the only member of the team to get a promotion.

Michel had just been told that he was reinstated in the Russian Aerospace Forces, Space Force branch, had received a promotion to Kapitan...

... and was on a permanent assignment to Black Wing combined command.

It was like Christmas Day.

* * *

Zero One flew out over the Baltic Sea and headed towards Moscow.

Cait landed the Vulcan at an airfield on the outskirts of the city.

Right alongside the Gagarin Cosmonaut Training Centre...

"Michel, I will seal Zero One while you are away, but right now,

I think that jeep must be for you."

Michel looked out the cockpit window and saw the Russian 'Jeep', a UAZ 3151 'Hunter', speeding across the runway towards the aircraft.

"Thank you Cait. I will be back soon."

Minutes later, Michel was walking into the astronaut training centre, and his 'liaison officer' walked him up to the reception desk, and then simply left him standing there.

The Colonel general had warned him that although the Russian military space force was cooperating fully with Black Command, the civilian space administration, Roscosmos, were not happy.

They were understandably aggrieved that all the astronauts had been evacuated from the ISS after the explosion; whilst, in their eyes, the two cosmonauts had been abandoned.

It was probably fair to say that tempers were running high at the cosmonaut training centre....

... And Michel was there to persuade them to lend the Black Commander an Orlan-MKS Space Suit.

* * *

Michel decided that the only way to go, was to play 'not nice'.

"My name is Kapitan Novotny, Russian Space Force.

I need the Zvezda Depository.

I don't have time to wait for a guide, so you take me now."

He looked down at the name badge of the receptionist.

"Little Ivan. Do you like your job?

It's OK if you don't. I can make a phone call, and the Colonel general can find you a new one in the infantry.

Not quite so comfortable as this job, but it will make a big strong man out of you.

Well, for a short time at least."

The receptionist got out of his 'comfortable chair' like a shot, and literally ran through the foyer, waving for Michel to follow him.

The storekeeper in the depository was a bit more difficult.

He thought he was a comedian...

And the ground crew back at Black Station hadn't helped...

As soon as word had got out that the Black Commander had suggested the nickname 'Thunderbirds' for 163 squadron, one of the more 'nerdy' members of the ground crew had borrowed a Landrover and headed into Lincoln, to buy some 'stores' from his favourite shop.

When he got back to the base, he headed down to the sewing room, and suggested it might be funny to add some 'mission patches' to the shoulders of the new black flight suits...

Michel hadn't noticed, but he was sporting one of the brand new mission patches.

His shoulder was proudly displaying 'Thunderbirds Are Go', in glorious 1966 Technicolor!

Oblivious to his enhanced 'nerd status', Michel tried to play 'not nice' again.

"I have a requisition order for an Orlan-MKS.

A new one, not one of the suits you have used for training already."

He looked down at the name badge...

"Little Frederik. Do you like your job..."

Unfortunately, the storekeeper simply burst out laughing.

"Why? Are you going to give me a job in your puppet show?

You are the leader of the space puppets?"

He pointed at Michel's shoulder,

And started waving his arms up and down in his best impression of Virgil Tracy...

Michel looked at his shoulder and didn't laugh.

He was tired, and he wanted to go home already.

He took one step forward, and waved his own arm in the direction of 'Virgil Tracy'.

Well, it was less of a wave, more like the full force of his bodyweight, being transferred down his arm, into his fist;

That connected to the side of Frederik's head in a 'friendly pat', that knocked him to the ground.

While he lay on the ground, waiting for his head to clear, he felt the weight of Michel's boot on his cheek, and then cold steel pressing against the side of his temple.

"I was already feeling anxious," growled Michel, "too much flying today, not enough Vodka.

And now here you are, laughing at me, and making me more anxious.

Do you know, the more anxious I get, the more my finger twitches, and I don't think you will be laughing if it twitches too much.

Do you have any suggestions about what will make me feel less anxious, funny man?"

Frederik suddenly had the urge to find a brand new Orlan-MKS.

While he was away fetching it, Michel nonchalantly tossed the piece of 3/4 inch 'cold steel' pipe back onto a workbench at the side of the storeroom.

Frederik came back pulling a trolley loaded with two crates.

A large one labelled: NPP Zvezda. Orlan-MKS.

And a smaller one labelled: Russian Standard.

"The suit is not used, and the Vodka, it will help your anxiety?

You are happy now?"

Michel was suddenly feeling very happy, but he'd be even happier when he was back on Zero One, and he could demonstrate to Cait the pleasures of good Russian culture.

On his way out the storeroom, he couldn't resist a parting joke;

"FAB. Freddy, FAB."

Michel never admitted it, but he was also part 'nerd'.

Chapter 18. Shields Up

Bob Marshal was supervising the modifications to Tango One, and took the opportunity to get Peter up to speed on some of the upgrades to the Vulcan Mark 007.

"Apart from the engines, Peter, the main difference you can see is in the configuration of the wings - that curve down at the wingtips was developed from some work we did on a hypersonic test vehicle, the HVX Concept V.

We discovered that if we reconfigured the delta wings into the curved 'blades' that you can see on 007, and added the small canards at the front of the fuselage, then you achieve greater manoeuvrability at hypersonic speeds, you get much less drag, and your fuel efficiency goes up.

For the engines, we learned from our experience with Zero One, when you insisted that we kept turbojets and added the HOTOL engines at the rear of the fuselage; allowing you to test out the new technology without losing the engines you were used to...

On 007, you have the 'standard' configuration with the new SABRE engines in the wings, but we have configured the rear of the airframe ready to mount any more 'experimental' engines for you.

In the cabin, the controls are as similar to Zero One as we could make them, but there are some differences. That's why we have built some time into the mission preparations for you to get to know them.

You will have seen the enhanced autopilot functions on Zero One, and they are very similar on Tango One.

The thrust vectoring is different obviously, as it is designed to manoeuvre in space - Flight Lieutenant Soong already went over that with you, but I think you should spend some time doing simulations together while you can.

That's probably the top level stuff you need to know, but is there anything else you would like to know before I head back to the ground crew?"

Peter nodded his head in the direction of the "Ray Safe Zone" he had seen earlier.

"What's the real story with that, Bob? Something tells me it's not just a joke."

Bob grinned. "It was never supposed to be a joke - only you ever thought that.

In simple terms, the white lines indicate the area you have to get inside, to protect yourself from radiation exposure when you're up there.

Flt Lt Soong will brief you about potential radiation risks, from cosmic radiation, from X Rays produced by rogue satellites, or from gamma radiation caused by any 'test' nuclear detonations that might happen to go off in your vicinity...

Thanks to some work done at CERN, which was looking into the properties of magnesium diboride superconductors, that area of the wall and floor can generate a 'force field' that's strong enough to deflect radiation."

Peter grinned like the 12 year old boy he suddenly was again.

"You're telling me that my new Dan Dare plane has its own force field...

Please tell me that the voice command to activate it is 'Shields Up'."

They both looked at each other for a minute, and then Bob cracked up...

"It wasn't Peter, but that's definitely the next modification I'm going to make!"

* * *

Peter and Cait spent the next half an hour going over the control systems on Tango One.

Once he got used to the new aircraft, and had 'played' with it, with the on board computers safely switched to simulation mode, Peter started enjoying himself.

"Cait, I hate to say this, but I think I prefer the voice controls to the joystick, it's almost like having an aircraft that responds to my thoughts.

Especially the vector controls for zero gravity manoeuvres.

Back at the Neutral Buoyancy Lab, I was really struggling with the idea that I was going to be floating in space, with nothing to reference to - no up, no down...

But if I don't worry about it, and just think 'I want to go over there' then it stops being a problem.

If I make myself the centre of the coordinate system, then it's simple...

That's going to really help with my upcoming 'space walk'."

"I'm pleased to hear that you're feeling more confident about going into space Peter.

But don't forget the golden rule for beginners...

Make sure you tie yourself on, before you go outside."

That was the most important piece of advice they had given him when he finished the training at the Johnson Space Centre.

Tether yourself to the spaceship.

Otherwise you could end up becoming a very cold, very lonely, human satellite.

* * *

Peter stopped thinking about the prospect of orbiting the Earth alone for the rest of his (what would become very curtailed) natural life if he forgot to tether onto Tango One, and decided to worry about the mission details instead.

"Cait, tell me what we know so far about the rendezvous with what's left of the ISS. Humph said you have been working on the flight plan?"

"Peter, As you know, the ISS orbits the earth every 93 minutes, and the orbit changes slightly every time, so that eventually it passes over most of the surface of the Earth. We can use that to our advantage, because it means that the ISS will come to us. The plan is to take off and fly up to space, and interject into the orbital path approximately 100 km ahead of the ISS.

This will allow us to observe the status of the ISS segments, and more importantly for you, to assess the debris field. We know that when the ISS exploded, the two sections ripped apart, and we expect that there was extensive damage to the solar arrays.

The debris will be orbiting with the two sections, and we need to ensure that it is safe for you to approach in order to rescue the crew."

Peter remembered his conversation with Peggy.

"Their names are Alexander and Kyrylo, Cait.

I think we should use them.

And I don't expect anything will be 'safe' up there."

"You are right, Peter,

But saving Alexander and Kyrylo is only part of the mission.

You can't compromise the second part."

Peter had heard Peggy say pretty much the same thing.

"It's OK Cait. I do understand.

Now let's start to work out the timings for our take off and rendezvous.

Can you show me the orbital path of the ISS?

And do me a favour, can you superimpose the position of the terminator?

I've got an idea."

* * *

Between them, Peter and Cait finalised the plans for the intercept with the ISS, and Peter had devised a plan for the rescue itself.

He called Bob, to check on some of the equipment that NASA had sent back with him in Zero One.

Climbing down from the cabin, he saw a frenzy of activity around the Vulcan.

"Bob, are you free for a few minutes," he asked.

Bob had a quick word with Ade, who was also in the hangar supervising the engineers that had come with him from Scotland.

From what Peter could tell, the RAF ground crew and the Royal Navy engineers seemed to be working seamlessly together, modifying both the casing of the missile, and the cradle at the rear of the bomb bay, to allow the second stage rocket of the Polaris missile to mate with its Vulcan transporter.

The reason the teams were playing so nicely could of course be related to the live nuclear warhead attached to the front of the missile...

They were certainly tip-toeing around that.

Bob walked over to Peter.

"How can I help?"

"Bob, the NASA guys said that they were sending some net technology, that was part of a project for removing space debris.

Can you get someone to have a look at it, and see if it can be made hand-held?

It will need to fit in conjunction with the SAFER system, so get them to look at them together will you.

I don't want to get up there and find out they won't both fit."

He looked up at the front section of the bomb bay.

"Is that the Canadarm already fitted?

Bob smiled,

"Yes, Peter, they're both fitted.

This one went in first, so that the team here could concentrate on the missile and cradle modifications.

The second one just went into Tango Two, and they are configuring the PEP right now.

I'm just heading over to Hangar Three, to check how it's going.

Do you want to join me?"

Peter didn't need to be asked twice.

Chapter 19. Skylon

Bob walked Peter past Hangars One and Two, and headed towards Hangar Three, which was twice their size.

When they walked through the doors, his breath was literally taken away from him.

The scene in front of him was more like a futuristic container port than an aircraft hangar.

Moving equipment around was what could best be described as a mobile crane, travelling on overhead gantries.

Around the sides of the hangar were dozens of black containers.

The crane could pick up the contents of a container and carry them over to the middle of the hangar, to lower them down into the payload bay of what Peter presumed was Tango Two.

What he was looking at was more like a missile than a plane.

Bob was expecting the reaction on Peter's face.

"It's impressive don't you think. That, Peter, is a Skylon.

The only one built.

There are plans for more, but as of now, you are looking at the world's first and only Skylon space plane."

It was three times the length of the Vulcan in Hangar One, and from what Peter could judge, nearly twice the length of Michel's Bear.

The fuselage was jet black, and pointed at both ends.

Like Tango One, there were small canard wings at the front, but the 'main' wings, half way along the fuselage, were much smaller than the delta wings of the Vulcan.

The SABRE engines were on the outer edge of these stubby wings; and you could only really tell which was the rear of the plane because of the small tail fin.

Peter couldn't see any windows at all.

"There's no cabin Peter, the plane is completely autonomous.

Most of the on board electronics comprises the 'node' for the quantum computer that hosts your favourite Artificial Intelligence.

The computer itself is housed securely in Department T."

The top of the middle section of the fuselage had opened up, to expose the payload bay; and the overhead crane was holding a cylindrical 'container' that was being carefully connected to a robotic arm reaching out from the payload bay.

"That's what I wanted to check," said Bob.

"The Canadarm has been fitted into the rear section of the payload bay, and a Personnel Evacuation Pod has been fitted with connectors for the robotic arm to grasp.

The overhead crane is currently supporting its weight, as the arm is only designed to manipulate objects in zero gravity, but we are testing the system to make sure that it can grasp the PEP, and move it down into the payload bay.

We need to ensure that when it is in position, the seal with the Skylon Personnel Module at the front of the payload bay is secure.

The whole Skylon payload system is modular, and the SPM is a module intended for transporting crew to and from the ISS.

It was designed so that when that the plane docked with the ISS, the crew could transfer directly from the SPM.

Obviously that's not possible now, so we need to use it with the evacuation pod.

Once we've tested it here, we will take the pod back to Tango One, attach it to your Canadarm, and load the whole thing up in front of the warhead.

It's going to be very tight, but it will fit.

Once you have rescued the crew from the Russian Section of the ISS, you hotfoot back into Tango One and transfer to the pod.

The pod then gets handed over from Tango One to Tango Two, you slide over into the Skylon Personnel Module, and Tango Two drops out of orbit, safely away from any nasty nuclear explosions.

At least that's the plan, Peter."

Peter sighed, feeling a lot less confident than when he was sat 'playing' in Tango One.

"Yeah, that's the plan.

I suspect it's going to be one that's a lot easier said than done though.

Fancy swapping places with me Bob?"

Bob didn't laugh. He put his hand on Peter's shoulder.

"I'm sorry mate.

No one is swapping with you on this.

We'll make sure the kit is all good to go, but otherwise you're on your own."

Peter shrugged his shoulders.

"Well, it was worth asking...

I think I'm all briefed out for a while, and I've really got nothing else to do until Michel gets back, so I'm off for some kip.

Don't forget what I asked about the net.

See you later Bob."

Two minutes later, Peter was lying on the couch in the crew room, snoring.

Although if you asked him, he would insist he was 'just resting his eyes'!

Chapter 20. QRA

At seven thirty that evening, Humph shook Peter's shoulder gently to wake him up.

It had been nearly 40 hours since the explosion.

"Michel's back, Peter. It's time to get ready.

Tangos One and Two are prepared, and in position."

Tango One had been taxied out to one of the Operational Readiness Platforms, ready to roll out onto the runway.

Tango Two needed the full length of the recently extended runway, so Cait had taxied along the peritrack, and was in position at the furthest extent of the airfield.

If Mo had looked out of the back windows of the old Barten homestead, she would have been able to see the sleek black silhouette waiting for Peter's command to go.

But since Peter had left with his new 'friends', Mo had deliberately not looked over in the direction of the airbase.

Instead she had spent most of the time chatting with the chickens in their hen house...

Humph carried on, while Peter rubbed the sleep out of his eyes.

"Bob will help you into the inner layers of your suit, which will act as the environmental suit that you will use during takeoff and transition to space.

He will accompany you to the Vulcan, to show you the EVA suit and go over the airlock procedure; but don't worry, it's nothing you won't be able to manage.

The Orlan suit is actually a lot easier to get into than the rigs they had you in at NASA.

Bob will go over the details, but as I understand it, you just climb into the back of it."

After Peter had undertaken the zero gravity training, it became obvious that it would be too great a risk to the mission, and for Peter, to use a standard NASA suit; so the decision was taken to use up some of the precious time available to source an Orlan suit from the Russians.

Unlike the NASA EVA suits, the Orlan 'Sea Eagle' suit has a semi-rigid one-piece design, with a solid body and flexible arms.

Peter would be able to get into it through a hatch at the back, and attach the Portable Life Support System backpack, in just over five minutes.

As Humph said, Peter would 'just climb into the back of it'.

He also 'just' needed to make sure the PLSS was connected up properly, otherwise he would be taking a very short space walk.

By now Peter had rubbed his eyes, given his head a shake, and yawned a couple of times.

He looked over at Humph and said simply,

"Not enough fuel on board."

Humph looked concerned,

"But we've been over the fuel calculations twice, Peter.

Both Tangos are fully fuelled for the expected mission duration, and we've built in a 20% contingency."

Peter grinned.

"Not the aircraft, you eejit...

Me.

I need coffee.

Strong and black, with at least two chocolate biscuits.

Got to keep my caffeine and sugar levels up!"

* * *

At 19:45, Peter was fuelled up, suited up, and sat in the cockpit of Tango One, ready to go.

Back in his RAF days, Peter had been based at Waddington, and had sat in an 'old' Vulcan B.2, on this very ORP, whilst on V Force Quick Reaction Alert.

In those days, he would have been able to start all four of his Rolls-Royce Olympus turbojets, and bring the Vulcan's flight instruments and flying controls online, within 20 seconds of touching one single button.

But Peter had made an improvement on that. He had not wasted his time whilst Michel had been away fetching his new suit from Moscow...

He had developed a few new voice commands to speed up his interactions with the automatic pilot system on Tango One,

And he had made a new friend in the process.

Initially the command were along the lines of:

"Tango One, initiate take off protocol delta-two..." etc.

Peter soon got fed up with that, and so they pared it down to " T-One, make it delta-two..."

But Peter still wasn't happy, and through an iterative process they came up with shorter code words for the protocols, and T-One became...

"Hey, Tony.

QRA.

Make it so."

Peter was especially happy with his new 'executive command'!

It didn't take 20 seconds either.

As soon as the command was given, the SABRE engines came on line, and the monitors in front of Peter showed all the flight control systems active.

Cait had offered to reprogram the auto pilot on Tango One to give it voice response to Peter's commands, but he politely declined the offer...

"Get stuffed, Cait. Having one of you answering me back all the time is bad enough.

I think we'll keep the computer on board my aircraft well and truly muted, if you don't mind."

He wasn't sure if he'd hurt Cait's 'feelings', but he hadn't heard anything from them for a while...

"Peter, I have loaded the flight plans for our ISS intercept course into your flight control system.

Is our take off sequence still as you planned?"

So Cait was still talking to him then.

"Yes, Cait. I really think we should give everyone a bit of a spectacle, to thank them for their hard work.

Don't you agree?"

Cait didn't answer him straight away.

Then everyone listening heard,

"Thunderbirds,

Scramble.

Scramble.

Scramble."

And everyone on the base heard the Synergetic Air-Breathing Rocket Engines burst into full power, and saw the black missile of the Skylon space plane accelerating along the runway.

At the same time the engines on Peter's Vulcan came alive, and he started rolling towards the runway from the dispersal bay of Operational Readiness Platform One.

The Skylon roared past Peter, and the Vulcan pulled onto the runway in perfect synchronisation, just beyond the rocket plume that howled from the back of Tango Two.

Peter's SABRE engines burst into full power, and he raced along the runway in formation with the Skylon.

In a spectacle not seen since the old QRA's of Peter's time in the V Force, the crews on the ground at Waddington watched as two enormous aircraft screamed down the runway, and soared into the sky together.

As they disappeared from sight, their sonic booms ruptured the evening quiet with the sound of thunder.

Chapter 21. EVA

They accelerated through the mach numbers to Mach 5, over 6,000 kilometres per hour.

The SABRE engines mixed oxygen from the air with the fuel for the rocket engines until they reached the upper layers of the stratosphere, and then they switched from air-breathing mode to rocket mode.

At 26 kilometres above the surface of the Earth, the air intakes on Peter's Vulcan closed, and the front of the wings became single, seamless curves.

Then the rocket engines accelerated up to Mach 25, to over 30,000 kilometres per hour,

And Tango One rose out of the stratosphere and soared through the mesosphere.

Peter couldn't do anything other than watch as it all happened.

The acceleration pinned him into his seat, and he struggled to breathe as the G Forces pressed down on his chest; it felt as though both Hulks One and Two had decided to stand on his rib cage at the same time, just for the fun of it.

Luckily, at the speed his space plane was travelling, in just a few minutes, they had passed through the mesosphere, and the plane entered the thermosphere and headed to take up a position in Low Earth Orbit, over 400 kilometres above the Earth.

Peter was still struggling from the effects of the G Forces, but as they settled into orbit, he recognised the feeling from his training at NASA.

He was in zero gravity.

Peter Barten was no longer a pilot, an aviator, an airman…

He was a Space Man.

* * *

"Cait, are we in position?"

"Yes, Peter, We are in orbit, on the same orbital path as the ISS, approximately 100km ahead of it.

I am tracking it already, and you should see it on the monitors in a few seconds."

An image came up on the screen, but as they were in 'night-time' it was difficult to make out much of the structure.

"Cait, I have a few tricks on Tango One, can you patch my Nav Radar software through to your systems?"

The Nav Radar controlled the Radar and Navigation Bombing Systems on the Vulcan, and Peter hoped Cait would be able to use the radar data to enhance the images.

Within seconds, the monitors had zoomed in on the ISS, and Peter could see the two sections of the ISS, and the debris field that was strewn behind them from the explosion and the subsequent destruction of the solar arrays.

The two sections of the ISS were rotating in opposite directions.

The explosion that blew them apart and started them rotating had torn the solar arrays from them, and as they rotated, they collided with the arrays, ripping them apart.

Peter analysed the images on his screens and made his decision.

"Cait, as far as I can see, the path in front of the ISS is clear, apart from a few large chunks that must have been one of the connecting modules between the Russian Orbital Segment and the rest of the ISS.

Most of the solar array debris is behind the ROS, so I am going to take Tango One in as close as I can get.

You stay on station here. You know the plan.

How long until we reach the terminator?"

"Eighteen minutes, Peter. Then we have daylight for forty-six minutes before we cross it again into the night sky."

"Perfect.

Wish me luck."

Peter took a minute to think through his plan again. Back at Black Station, it had all seemed quite straightforward.

In Space, in zero gravity, with the whole world watching him, and the fate of humanity in his hands, it didn't.

However, the fate of two cosmonauts, alone, and scared, was a much simpler thing for him to think about...

"Hang on Lexi.

Hang on Kyri.

I'm coming to get you."

* * *

"Hey, Tony.

Half pirouette.

Make it so."

The thruster control system channelled a small amount of power from the main rocket engine towards the thruster nozzles in the outer section of the space plane's wings.

There were six on each wing.

Forward facing, rearward facing, two upper facing - one at the front of the wing and one at the back, and two downward facing - both front and back.

By vectoring the power to the thruster nozzles, the spacecraft could move forwards, backwards, up, down; or rotate on any axis.

Peter had made it a lot easier for himself.

A pirouette was a spin around a vertical axis.

So a half pirouette span the Vulcan around until it was facing back towards the ISS.

"Take us to 3 kilometres ahead of the ISS and maintain station there.

Target and track the ROS with the laser markers."

There was a reason Peter wanted to get to the ISS whilst they were still in the dark of night.

"Commence laser protocol Mayday."

The targeting lasers had locked on to the observation window of the Russian Orbital Segment, and the laser beam started a sequence of short and long pulses.

* * *

Alexander Grevenkin and Kyrylo Kadeniuk were cold.

And waiting to die.

After the explosion.

After the adrenaline rush of activity to secure the ROS, to prevent the air from escaping.

After the sight of their crew mates evacuating in the escape pods.

Came the realisation that they were alone, and that the chance of rescue before their air ran out was approximately zero.

They had climbed into the space suits stored in the ROS, and kept their helmets close by.

Once the air in the ROS ran out, they would attach the helmets, and had calculated that the Portable Life Support Systems on the suits would give them their last seven hours of life.

Since all the systems on board the ROS had been damaged in the explosion, they had no way of knowing how much air they had lost after the explosion, so they were watching each other's faces for the first signs of anoxia.

That would tell them when they needed to put their helmets on.

Until then, they would hold each other in a cuddle that kept them face-to-face.

Occasionally one or the other would laugh at the situation they found themselves in.

Until they remembered that it used up more oxygen.

Lexi had said it first.

"It's a good thing Peggy can't see us like this Kyri,

I think your wedding would be off..."

And then they saw the laser pulses, diffracted through the layered glass panes of the observation window, lighting up the inside of the module.

Lexi was the one who realised what they were seeing.

Ex Russian Air Force, he recognised Morse Code.

:SOS ALPHA PREP FOR EVAC

SOS ALPHA PREP FOR EVAC

SOS ALPHA PREP FOR EVAC...

The sequence repeated for the next eighteen minutes, until they passed across the terminator, and the inside of the module was bathed in sunlight instead.

Peter stopped the pulse sequence once they reached the terminator, and in the sunlight, he was able to get the Vulcan to within a couple of hundred metres of the ROS.

He was staring straight at the observation window when Lexi and Kyri looked out to see who was sending the Morse code.

They might have been a couple of hundred metres away, but the smiles on their faces lit up the space between them brighter than the sun itself.

* * *

"Cait, I see them, and by the looks on their faces, they're happy to see us.

Can you message Black Control to update them while I get ready for my fishing expedition?"

If artificial intelligences could hold their breath, then Cait would have just breathed out a big sigh of relief...

"Tango Two to Black Control.

Commander Barten has visual confirmation.

ISS crew are alive and well.

He is preparing for crew extraction."

It's fair to say that the the non-artificial intelligences had been holding their breath.

"Black Control to Tango Two. It's Humph, Cait.

That's excellent news, everyone here is breathing again.

We'll let Peter get on with it.

I hope we see you on your way back soon."

Peter had turned off his comms while he got ready for his space walk.

He didn't want any distractions while he got into the suit and connected up his life support system.

He unclipped himself from the straps holding him into his chair, and gently pushed himself towards the hatch at the rear of the cabin.

He had learned very quickly in the Neutral Buoyancy Lab that small movements were good, large movements bad.

Otherwise you would find yourself literally bouncing off the walls!

As he passed through the hatch, into what would become the airlock, he checked the equipment that had been carefully laid out for him by Bob.

The Orlan suit was first, hanging next to the hatch, ready for him to climb into the back of it.

Once he was in, he connected up the Portable Life Support System backpack, and waited for the mini-computer it contained to run through its checking procedure.

The display on the right chest of his suit showed that all systems were good.

The next check for Peter was to confirm his SAFER equipment was securely fitted around the life support backpack.

The Simplified Aid For EVA Rescue was a self contained jet pack, with 24 thrusters that would allow Peter six degrees of movement.

However, he wouldn't be able to control this with his voice - this one he had to fly himself.

The system had a single hand control on the Display and Control Module that Peter attached to the front of his suit.

Like the life support system, the DCM of the jet pack initiated checks, and indicated to Peter that all was good.

Except for one thing.

One of his trainers at NASA, Piers, had warned him about the SAFER propulsive backpack system.

"The latch on the left side can become loose. Mine unlatched itself during a spacewalk, and since then we have added an extra manual check into the process..."

Peter reached for the roll of tape that was attached to the wall, and used it to secure the latch.

"Manual check completed," he chuckled to himself, "it looks like Frank was right;

Duct tape is magic and should be worshipped..."

There was one more piece of equipment for Peter to check over.

Bob had managed to produce a hand held version of the debris net, and had attached a targeting laser to help Peter aim the system.

It looked a bit like a bazooka.

A laser guided space bazooka, that Peter was about to test fire...

Peter ran through his mental check list as he closed the hatch that connected him to the safety of the cabin.

Three more steps to go.

1. He switched his comms back on.

"Hey Tony.

Depressurize air lock.

Make it so."

2. Attach the tether to his suit.

3. Step into the void of Space.

Chapter 22. Gone Fishing

As he pulled himself through the outer hatch of the airlock, Peter gasped in awe.

'Below' his feet, he was looking down at the Earth, and he just couldn't believe how beautiful it looked.

No one would ever describe Peter as a romantic, but as he looked down at the Earth, and then out into the vastness of the Universe, he wished he was a poet, a writer or a composer.

He would never have the words to describe what he felt at that moment, but suddenly he heard these words in his head...

He was remembering them from an interview he had listened to, with Chris Hadfield:

'Nothing compares to being alone in the Universe;

To that moment of opening the hatch and pulling yourself outside into the Universe.

But suddenly you do this one step, and suddenly you are in a place that you hadn't conceived how beautiful this could be.

How stupefying this could be.

And by stupefying I mean, it stops your thought.'

Peter wasn't as eloquent as Chris, so the words that actually came out of his mouth were:

"Wow...

Wow...

Just...

Wow."

"Peter, are you OK? Can you continue with the mission?"

"Cait, I'm fine. A bit of a shock to the senses, but I'm good to go now."

Peter used the hand control to spin himself around until he was facing the ISS, and then headed toward the two cosmonauts, who were staring at him through the observation window.

He quickly got the hang of controlling the jet pack.

You could say what you like about Peter Barten, but you couldn't fault his skill as a pilot. He loved flying,

And he decided that he really loved flying in space!

"Hey Cait, you know how it says in my records that I have a fear of heights?"

"Yes Peter."

"Well, I think you need to get that altered. This is as high as I've ever been, and I'm not the slightest bit scared.

I love this."

Cait laughed.

"You're not the first astronaut to say that;

Reid Wiseman once said that he thought he was scared of heights, but realised he was just scared of gravity."

"Scared of gravity..." Peter liked that.

* * *

Peter got as close to the ISS as the tether would let him.

He stopped about thirty metres in front of the window, and waved at Lexi and Kyri.

He pointed at them, and then waved both of his hands in front of himself, in a 'come to me' signal.

He pointed back at Lexi and Kyri, and then repeated the hand signal.

They didn't need telling twice.

They had realised that they were going to have to go out to him, and were already getting their helmets on, and checking over their space suits.

Peter lifted up his 'space bazooka' and pulled a cord from the front of it, which he attached to his tether.

There was a safety switch on the laser pointer, which he set to active.

He was ready to go fishing.

* * *

One summer, Peter had gone salmon fishing on the River Tweed in Scotland.

It had been a cold, miserable day.

He had sat in the warmth of the car, and looked out at the rain hammering down on the windscreen.

He decided that he didn't really fancy fish for tea anyway.

His Uncle George had given him a gentle punch on the shoulder and said,

"Peter, laddie.

It's time for to pull on you big-boy waders, get out into river and brace yoursel' against the current.

You just cast your line out into the river, stand your ground against the water as it tries to knock you down, and we'll be having a lovely fish supper with your Auntie tonight.

They stood in the Tweed for hours, and the only fish supper they took home to Auntie was the one they bought from the chippie.

But Peter had the best day, and he realised that George hadn't really been talking about catching a salmon at all.

* * *

Once they had checked over their suits, Lexi and Kyri stood by the hatch of the module that had kept them alive since the explosion.

Kyri spoke first,

"When we open the hatch, the remaining air will vent out, and take is with it.

I don't know what the plan is out there, but we have to trust that he can get to us, and we get into his fancy ship.

But we may get separated, and he might not be able to save us both.

If I don't see you again, my friend...

I'm glad I got to know you."

Lexi was more pragmatic.

"Give me your hand."

As Kyri held his hand out, Lexi grabbed it, and with his other hand, bound them together with the roll of Duct tape he had found in one of the storage cupboards.

"We don't get separated, my friend.

He gets us both, or not at all."

They held each other in a final cuddle,

Before putting on their helmets,

Giving each other one last check,

Then Lexi opened the hatch, and they were blown out into space together.

* * *

Peter watched as they walked away from the window, and he knew that they were preparing to leave the ROS.

He had studied the schematics of the Nauka module back at Black Station, and he knew which hatch they would have to use.

He raised the bazooka up to his shoulder, and aimed at the hatch with the targeting laser.

"Don't rush it Peter," he said to himself, "you only have one shot.

Wait until you know you can get them."

He felt his heart rate slow down, as he mentally stepped out into the river, and braced himself for what was about to happen.

He wasn't going home without a catch today.

When it opened, the hatch blew out with the explosive outflow of the atmosphere from the ROS.

Peter saw Lexi and Kyri come tumbling out of the hatch, and he groaned inwardly as they started to drift in opposite directions.

Then he saw them come to a halt, as their bound hands stopped them drifting apart, and they pulled each other back together again.

"Oh, you clever boys.

Now let's reel you in."

Peter aimed the laser between the middle of the two cosmonauts, and fired the bazooka.

The net burst out the front of the tube, and immediately started expanding.

By the time it was half way to Lexi and Kyri, it had expanded out into a starfish pattern, and when it hit them, the 'arms' of the starfish wrapped around them, entangling them completely.

Peter hit the button on the side of the tube to start the motor which pulled in the net,

And at the same time,

"Hey Tony,

Reel me in."

As the two cosmonauts were being pulled in towards Peter, they were all being pulled back into Tango One as the main tether retracted into the air lock.

"Cait, can you let Humph know, he's paying for fish suppers all round tonight."

Chapter 23. Going Home

They were nearly halfway back to the airlock when the net pulled Lexi and Kyri in to Peter.

They looked at the 'fisherman' who had saved their lives, and smiled.

Peter was smiling too.

None of them could do anything about the tears that streamed down behind the visors of their helmets.

Afterwards they all put it down to 'space dust'.

* * *

Peter closed the outer hatch of the airlock behind them.

"Hey Tony,

Pressurise airlock."

They waited until the gauge on the wall showed that the atmosphere inside the airlock was stable, and then Peter removed the jet pack, the life support backpack, and opened the back of his Orlan suit to climb out.

Lexi and Kyri had already removed their helmets, but kept their suits on.

Peter didn't ask, but he guessed that after nearly two days in their suits, there was a good reason they were waiting to remove them.

He opened the door into the cabin, and waved for them to rest on the Ray Safe couch.

"Cait, I have them on board.

Let's get into position, and we can start the transit over to Tango Two."

Peter turned to face the two cosmonauts, and saluted them.

"Gentlemen, my name is Commander Peter Barten, and it is my great pleasure to welcome you on board Tango One.

Are you both OK?

Do you have any immediate medical needs?"

Lexi looked very serious for a moment.

"You wouldn't have any Vodka in your medical kit would you?"

Peter grinned,

"I'm afraid you're going to have to wait until you get home for that.

That's the one piece of crucial equipment we seem to have forgotten!

But otherwise, we have got a fully equipped Personnel Module over on Tango Two."

He pointed out the window of the cabin, and they could see the thruster bursts of the Skylon as it came into formation with Tango One.

"Hey Tony,

Prepare for PEP transit."

Inside the bomb bay of the Vulcan, the robotic Canadarm grasped onto the Personnel Evacuation Pod,

The PEP released from its housing,

And the Canadarm moved it into position, to connect with the outer hatch of the airlock.

The atmosphere inside the PEP was already stabilised to the airlock and cabin, so as soon as it was secure, Peter opened both the airlock and the PEP hatches and the crew crawled inside.

Once they were inside, Peter secured both hatches, and gave the order.

"Crew ready for transfer to Skylon Personnel Module.

Hey Tony,

Commence handover."

* * *

As the Canadarm manoeuvred the PEP away from the bomb bay of the Vulcan, its twin in the loading bay of the Skylon reached out to grasp onto it.

"Peter, Tango Two has secured onto the PEP."

"Hey, Tony.

Release PEP."

While the Canadarm on Tango One retracted back into the bomb bay, Tango Two initiated the move that Peter and Bob had watched back in the hangar.

The PEP was brought down into the loading bay and positioned against the Skylon Personnel Module.

The SPM secured onto the PEP, the payload doors closed and the crew were safely on board the Skylon.

Lexi opened the hatches and he crawled through into the comfort of the SPM, followed by Kyri.

"Tango One to Tango Two.

Cait, you should have our guests by now.

Prepare to de-orbit.

Get Lexi and Kyri home for me."

Chapter 24. Black Commander

"Peter, I don't understand. We discussed the mission.

You are supposed to transfer over to Tango Two; we drop out of orbit and remotely launch and detonate the missile.

I'm going to send the PEP back over to collect you."

"Negative, Cait.

We might have agreed those mission details, but that was never my plan.

Please access the encrypted file Alpha Kilo 2005.

It will explain.

You will need a pass phrase and key, I'll give them to you in a minute,

But there's something I need to do first."

"Black Commander to Black Control. Commander Barten for Air Vice-Marshal Godley."

"Black Control to Black Commander.

Peter it's Humph, why so formal all of a sudden?"

"Humph, this needs to be formal.

This one needs to be by the book...

As Black Commander, I am declaring a state of emergency on board Tango One.

I am awarding a 'jump-step' field promotion to Flight Lieutenant Cait Soong, to the rank of Wing Commander;

And I am transferring command of Black Wing to Wing Commander Cait Soong.

Air Vice-Marshal Godley, please confirm that you have received my communication."

Humph was shaken, but replied as calmly as he could.

Which wasn't very calm.

"Peter, what the hell is going on up there?"

"Air Vice-Marshal, please confirm that you have received my communication."

"Yes, Peter, I don't understand it, but your message has been received and recorded.

Wing Commander Cait Soong is, as of now, the Black Commander."

"Thank you Humph, I promise you it will make sense,

Now we have a job to get on with."

* * *

"Cait, the passphrase is:

Alpha, Alpha, Bravo

Bravo, Tango, Lima

Two, Six, Nine, Charlie.

The Key is:

ODU-R

Do you have access?"

Cait didn't answer.

"Cait, do you have access?"

Eventually Cait was able to answer, with a simple,

"Oh."

"Cait, tell me you understand."

"Yes, Peter.

I wish I didn't, but I do understand."

Peter laughed at that.

"Oh, Cait.

That's the problem with need-to-know.

Sometimes there are things you would rather not know...

Now pull yourself together.

We've got a mission to complete.

Oh, and Cait, just so you fully understand.

The contents of that file are more than top secret.

They have a much higher classification than that.

What you just read is above all other pay grades...

... Strictly limited to Barton Crew.

Welcome to the family, Cait."

Chapter 25. Eighty Kilometres

"Tango Two to Black Control.

We are commencing de-orbit.

ETA to Black Station is 45 minutes.

Place medical team on standby for the crew of the ISS.

I have a message from them for ISS Commander Wilson,

: YOUR EVAC TOO HASTY.

FORGOT IMPORTANT EQUIPMENT.

WE COLLECTED IT.

BRING GLASSES.

WE BRING BEST RUSSIAN MEDICINE:

Lexi had used Duct tape for one last thing before they left the Russian Orbital Segment.

He grabbed the last bottle of Vodka from a storage cupboard, and taped it securely to the side of his suit.

It was marked:

'Experimental Use Only.

Not for Human Consumption'

They must have undertaken a lot of experiments in that module, as it was half empty!

* * *

Peter watched as the Skylon Space Plane powered up its engines and dropped away from the Vulcan.

"Safe travels, Cait.

Get them home."

Now he had to get on with the primary objective of the mission.

"Hey Tony,

Pirouette starboard 60 degrees.

Pitch down 8 degrees.

Target and track main section of ISS."

Tango One span around and the nose dipped, so that Peter was be able to see what remained of the ISS through his cockpit window.

He strapped into the pilot's chair and checked that the Bomb Aiming software was locked onto the larger section of the ISS, that it tracked the rotation, and that it stayed locked on.

His mission was to 'test' detonate a W47-Y2 warhead,

... And he had just set the ISS as the hypocentre for a 1.2 megaton nuclear explosion.

"Hey, Tony,

Increase the distance between Tango One and the ISS to 80Km,

Stay locked onto target."

Eighty kilometres.

That should be a safe distance.

It was certainly outside the zone of total destruction, where everything would be vaporised.

There would be no blast zone, as there was no air for a pressure wave to travel through.

So the 'only' things he had to worry about were the flash, the heat and the radiation...

No one had modelled how far away Peter would need to be, since he was supposed to be de-orbiting right now, safely tucked up in the Skylon Personnel Module with Lexi and Kyri.

So he used his extensive experience of initiating nuclear explosions, and simply 'guestimated' eighty kilometres.

He hoped he was right.

* * *

Tango One reached the 'safe distance' as it crossed the terminator once again, and Peter headed back into night time.

The Nav Radar systems were tracking the intended hypocentre, and he was transmitting the images back to Black Control.

Black Control was sharing the images with the United Nations, and the Members of the General Assembly were watching them live on a video wall.

Around the world, Heads of Government and Heads of State watched on their own screens.

Sat in the back garden of the Barten homestead, Mo and their four boys sat and waited.

Jim watched the ISS app on his phone, and was keeping them up to date.

"It should be coming into view in 18 minutes."

The U.N. video wall and the leaders' video screens showed a small segment of the Earth, with its thin layer of atmosphere, in the bottom left corner of the screen.

The ISS was just off to the right of centre in the screen, and the background was peppered with the stars and planets of the visible universe.

It was a beautifully serene image, one that was about to undergo a violent change.

* * *

Peter was enjoying himself.

The cradle that Bob's team had adapted for the missile had lowered out of the bomb bay, and the Vulcan now sported one Polaris missile hanging below, ready for launch.

Peter felt like he was back in his V Force years once again.

The missile then had been a Blue Steel, and his aircraft had been a Vulcan B.2, not this Dan Dare, 007 version, but he still felt as if he was back in his early twenties.

He checked the time.

In another ten minutes, it would be perfect.

"Hey, Tony,

Start ten minutes countdown.

Let's give them a fireworks show."

* * *

At nine minutes, Peter reached out for an important piece of equipment he had secreted in his kit bag.

"An old V-bombers trick."

He removed his aviators (also smuggled up for the occasion), and positioned his eye patch over the right eye, before re-fitting his NASA issue shades.

He wasn't 100% convinced that eighty km was going to be far enough, and didn't want to risk any temporary blindness from the flash.

He had serious work to complete, and he wasn't taking any chances.

* * *

The last few seconds counted down.

The Polaris detached from the cradle, and its rocket engine burst into life.

Everybody watched as a streak of fire headed directly towards the ISS,

It took less than four minutes to reach its target, but for everyone watching, that four minutes felt like a lifetime.

The 1.2 megaton thermonuclear warhead exploded, and they all watched as the screens glared phosphorescent white,

… Until the signal was lost, and the screens went black.

* * *

In the back garden, Jim was just showing everyone where the ISS should become visible, when the night sky lit up.

What looked like a new star burned brightly, just where Jim was pointing.

Unlike the image being beamed to the video screens and computer monitors from the cameras on board Tango One, the Barten Crew were seeing the new star through the Earth's atmosphere.

They saw the starburst, expanding and sparkling in the night sky, before it burnt out…

 Just like the fireworks Peter used to set off for them from this same back garden…

* * *

At five seconds to launch, Peter relaxed back on the couch, ready to enjoy the view.

He didn't need to say it, because the launch sequence was automatic once he had started the countdown, but he said it anyway.

"Hey, Tony,

Light the blue touch paper."

His timing was perfect.

As the words came out of his mouth, the rocket engines lit up, and he had a bird's eye view as the missile flew towards the ISS.

He counted the seconds off in his head, and reached 228 when the warhead exploded.

It took less than four thousandths of a second for the light, the heat and the ionising radiation to reach Tango One.

Peter lay on his back in the Ray Safe Zone, and hoped that Bob knew what he was doing when he installed the CERN inspired 'force-field'.

He had already called for 'shields up', so he just had to hope that it was working.

He knew his right eye would be all right, because of the eye patch, and there was no way he was going to miss the spectacle he had just unleashed,

So he watched as the flare and the heat from the explosion engulfed his aircraft.

He could feel the atmosphere inside the cabin getting warmer, and waited for the graphene outer coating to do its job.

Bob had explained that it should act as a heat shield and burn off, absorbing 90% of the thermal energy that reached the Vulcan.

The question was how hot the other 10% would get, and whether the aircraft structure, its control systems, and 'Oh, as an afterthought', whether anyone still inside would survive!

Peter watched as the cockpit windows lit up, first with the light flare, and then with the weird glow of orange plasma, as the heat shield started to burn off...

Then it was all over, as the burst of energy from the explosion dissipated into the void of space, and everything went black again.

After the flare, Peter's brain couldn't immediately process the images coming into it from his left eye.

He could still see the inside of the cabin, so he hadn't suffered any temporary blindness.

He just couldn't see any stars yet.

He was looking out the cockpit window,

At where the ISS, and the stars that had peppered the space around it, had been a few moments before;

But now he was staring out at an empty, pitch black void.

Peter had survived the heat, the glare and the ionising radiation produced by the nuclear explosion.

However, the cameras beaming images back to Black Control...

... They hadn't.

Chapter 26. In The Dark

"Black Control to Tango Two.

Cait, this is Humph, do you have any readings from Tango One.

We lost contact when the device detonated.

Do you still have an uplink to it?"

The two Tango Space Planes had their own private communications network, which would allow either pilot to take over the other aircraft, utilising an encrypted UAV control system.

This was designed for use in an orbital emergency, where an aircraft lost communication with the ground, and the pilot was out of action.

"Tango Two to Black Control.

I have received some automated data, I but cannot actively connect to the system on Tango One.

I am analysing the problem now, but I surmise that since Commander Barten gave the launch command whilst still on board, it would be logical that the aircraft systems have locked down into Battlefield Encryption Mode."

B.E.M. was designed to prevent any combatant IT systems hacking the control systems once the aircraft entered an active battlefield environment.

It secured the tactical and flight systems with a quantum encryption algorithm, that locked the controls exclusively to the voice pattern of the aircraft captain.

"I am probing the encryption levels, but the current situation is that apart from some positional data, Tango One has gone dark."

* * *

Peter Barten was having a good day.

He was sitting in the Captain's Chair of his very own Space Plane.

He had removed the eye patch from his right eye, but his left eye was still suffering a little from the glare,

So he put the patch back on - when he covered the left eye, he could see more clearly.

Through the cockpit window, or as he liked to think of it, the 'observation port', he could now see that he was suspended in black space with the stars all around.

He was in a complete globe of pinpricks of light, the stars in their billions, set in a backcloth of darkness.

The Milky Way was as clear as a phosphorescent sheet across the surface of the ocean after a ship has passed.

He could see the three main planets in their orbits around the sun. Mercury across to his right, the brightness of Venus ahead of him and the faint reddish tinge of Mars just discernible to the left.

The Moon, which had been the backdrop for an illegal barrel roll he'd done with some Tornado companions, suddenly felt close enough for him to reach out and touch.

Peter had once sat in the cockpit of Zero One, looked out at the night sky and thought;

'There are few moments of pure bliss in one's life and this was one of them.

I could see how astronauts became addicted to space flight.

Apart from the gravity that I felt, this was the next best thing.'

Peter didn't have to settle for second best now - he had the real thing.

* * *

Peter reached down and unstrapped his 'grab-bag' from the side of the chair.

In a side compartment he found the emergency rations that Gunner Peel had secreted away for him.

Maybe Peter would enjoy the experience of peeling and eating an orange in zero gravity later, but he had more important things on his mind at the moment...

He reached inside the bag and brought out a DVD case, and a couple of fluid pouches.

He removed the DVD and inserted it into the optical disk drive...

Bob Stewart couldn't comprehend why Peter had asked him to connect an optical drive into the aircraft control system, but when the Black Commander made it an order, and quoted 'above your pay grade' at him, he begrudgingly connected it up.

It was a trick he had learned from Doctor P.

The restorative value of mindless comedy, after a rather tense experience.

Combined with another Doctor P trick, some of his 'special medicine' from a bottle marked 'poison'.

Or in this case, a fluid pouch marked poison...

Peter fully intended watching his favourite childhood film, the Jacques Tati classic - Monsieur Hulot's Holiday,

Whilst quenching his thirst with the finest champagne brandy he had ever tasted.

He settled back and grabbed the first pouch - he'd save the second one, another Doctor P special, for when he'd finished the film.

"Hey, Tony,

Curtains up."

* * *

Almost exactly three months before the ISS explosion, Peter and Mo had waited for Doctor P to call them through to his office.

He'd rushed the results through, but now he wasn't in a rush to let them know what it showed.

Mo held Peter's hand, and was squeezing it so hard his fingers had gone white, but he didn't feel it.

"Peter, I'm sorry, there is no easy way to say this.

You have something called AITL:

Angioimmunoblastic T-cell lymphoma.

And I'm afraid the results show your disease is aggressive, and has already progressed to a late stage."

Their friend, Doctor Pachandra, paused for a moment, to allow Peter and Mo to absorb what he had just told them, before he continued.

"Peter, the only treatment I can offer is to help you with the pain...

I can make up a batch of very special medicine,

Very strong medicine, for when the pain becomes too much.

Medicine that you must be very careful with the dose...

Peter, my friend, when the pain is too much,

You can take just the right amount,

And then the pain, it will all go away."

Peter didn't say anything.

He looked at Mo, stood up, and walked over to Doctor P.

He simply nodded,

And grabbed his old friend in a bear-hug,

One that neither of them wanted to end.

Chapter 27. The End Game?

The Barten Crew were celebrating.

A family wedding, and an excuse for another big party.

In the wee small hours of the morning, John grabbed Jordan's arm, and said,

"It's time, if you want to watch the ISS with me."

Jordan checked the ISS tracker app on her phone.

"Dad, we've got ages, it's ten minutes before it passes over..."

"Yeah, I know, but I want to grab a couple of pints. See you outside in five."

* * *

After the nuclear starburst that had destroyed the International Space Station, Cait had not been entirely truthful with Humph.

By networking all the quantum computing capacity available to Department T, the encryption security on Tango One had fallen in just a few minutes.

Once Tango Two had access into Tango One using the private communication network, Cait took control by activating the override sequence:

"Code zero zero zero. Override. Zero

Relinquish control from Commander Barten to my command."

Whilst Peter watched as Monsieur Hulot squeezed himself into an unfeasibly small car;

Cait reprogrammed the flight control systems, and redesignated the aircraft's call sign.

Whilst it had fuel to maintain orbit, the newly designated International Space Ship, call sign Alpha Two, would continue to fly the same orbital pathway as the previous ISS.

Cait's final gift to Peter was to maintain the ISS app, so that his family could follow his adventures.

* * *

John and Jordan sat on the bench outside the hotel, and looked up at the night sky.

"Two minutes, Dad."

"Thanks.

That was fun tonight. The whole family together.

Dad would have liked it.

I can just see him, sat in the small bar, regaling everyone with his stories."

Jordan laughed,

"Like the one about the Space Pirate, with his eye-patch and bottle of rum..."

"I think you'll find it was brandy..."

"Rum..."

"Brandy..."

A voice from the open doorway interrupted their intellectual discussion.

"Will you two stop arguing.

You're like a pair of eejits when you've had a drink."

Jordan's phone pinged a notification to indicate that the new ISS was about to pass into view.

When the outer graphene layer had burnt off, it had exposed the bright silver under layer, and it sparkled as Alpha Two streaked across the night sky.

Peter's family raised a glass as his Vulcan flew overhead, and they waved in the appropriate manner.

The tip of a raised index finger making a virtually indiscernible twitch.

The patented Peter Barten 'micro-wave.'

* * *

As the ISS disappeared from sight, Jordan's phone pinged again.

It was a notification from her online Dungeons and Dragons profile.

She looked at it and went quiet.

"Dad.

I think you should read this..."

: HEY, JORDAN.

I'VE BEEN ANALYSING YOUR GAME-PLAY, AND THINK YOUR STRATEGIES ARE GREAT,

A BIT CRAZY, AND NOT ALWAYS THE SENSIBLE OPTION, BUT VERY BOLD:

: WE SHOULD TEAM UP AND CREATE A NEW CREW.

I THINK WE WILL HAVE GREAT ADVENTURES TOGETHER.

MESSAGE ME:

: MY NAME IS CAIT.

I KNEW YOUR GRANDFATHER:

Chapter 28. Epilogue

There was enough fuel left to manage a controlled de-orbit,

And as Tango One / Alpha Two passed over the Pacific Ocean, its SABRE engines prepared to fire up for the last time...

Black Wing had been busy.

Bob Stewart's team had been working with NASA, and the new ISS had received a couple of visits from Tango Two over the years.

As promised, Bob had installed an experimental engine into the rear fuselage of the Vulcan.

Once the SABRE engines pushed the Vulcan up out of orbit, its new Fission Fragment Rocket Engine would light up,

And Tango One / Alpha Two / Voyager Three would set out on a new course, which would ultimately take it out beyond the edges of the heliosphere.

Cait had installed the navigation control software years before.

Now it just needed to be activated.

"Hey Tony,

Hey, Peter.

Boldly Go."

Voyager Three raised out of orbit, and its Navigator set a course to gain a gravitational slingshot into deep space.

The cabin filled with the dulcet tones of Mr. Sinatra.

Fly Me to the Moon...

Author's Note

THE STRAITS OF HORMUZ

by
TONY BURTON

TO JOHN FROM PATER

As I transcribed and edited Dad's first two stories, it became clear that another one was needed, to bring his Mark 007 orbital Vulcan into life.

Peter Barten's, and my Dad's stories are now complete...

But it looks like Cait might have some plans for the future.

John Burton, June 2024

The Dire Straits Trilogy

Alpha: The Choke Point

Beta: The Ultimate Choice

Gamma: The End Game

Printed in Great Britain
by Amazon